W9-CFA-662

"Are you hurt?" Zach asked.

The worry and care in his voice and expression was so clear that it made her heart ache.

"I'm sorry—" she started.

"Don't you dare apologize," he said. "Someone attacked you in your home. Anyone would have been terrified."

"I was," she said, and looked down, almost embarrassed that she'd been so scared.

He placed his finger under her chin and tilted her head back up until she met his gaze. "But you fought back and got away," he said. "You're a strong, brave woman."

Her heart pounded in her throat and more than anything, she wanted him to kiss her. No matter how hard she'd tried to resist her attraction to Zach, her body always betrayed her. It came alive when he was close to her, as never before.

She felt her body lean forward, anticipating the kiss, but instead, he released her and scanned the cabin.

THE BETRAYED

USA TODAY Bestselling Author
JANA DeLEON

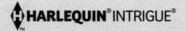

If you purchased this book without a cover you should be aware that this book is stolen property. It was reported as "unsold and destroyed" to the publisher, and neither the author nor the publisher has received any payment for this "stripped book."

Recycling programs
for this product may
not exist in your area.

To my husband, Rene, who always believed in me.

ISBN-13: 978-0-373-74768-9

THE BETRAYED

Copyright © 2013 by Jana DeLeon

All rights reserved. Except for use in any review, the reproduction or utilization of this work in whole or in part in any form by any electronic, mechanical or other means, now known or hereafter invented, including xerography, photocopying and recording, or in any information storage or retrieval system, is forbidden without the written permission of the publisher, Harlequin Enterprises Limited, 225 Duncan Mill Road, Don Mills, Ontario M3B 3K9, Canada.

This is a work of fiction. Names, characters, places and incidents are either the product of the author's imagination or are used fictitiously, and any resemblance to actual persons, living or dead, business establishments, events or locales is entirely coincidental.

This edition published by arrangement with Harlequin Books S.A.

For questions and comments about the quality of this book, please contact us at CustomerService@Harlequin.com.

® and TM are trademarks of Harlequin Enterprises Limited or its corporate affiliates. Trademarks indicated with ® are registered in the United States Patent and Trademark Office, the Canadian Trade Marks Office and in other countries.

Printed in U.S.A.

www.Harlequin.com

ABOUT THE AUTHOR

USA TODAY bestselling author Jana DeLeon grew up among the bayous and small towns of southwest Louisiana. She's never actually found a dead body or seen a ghost, but she's still hoping. Jana started writing in 2001—she focuses on murderous plots set deep in the Louisiana bayous. By day she writes very boring technical manuals for a software company in Dallas. Visit Jana on her website, www.janadeleon.com.

Books by Jana DeLeon

HARLEQUIN INTRIGUE
1265—THE SECRET OF CYPRIERE BAYOU
1291—BAYOU BODYGUARD
1331—THE LOST GIRLS OF JOHNSON'S BAYOU
1380—THE RECKONING*
1386—THE VANISHING*
1393—THE AWAKENING*
1441—THE ACCUSED**
1447—THE BETRAYED**

*Mystere Parish
**Mystere Parish: Family Inheritance

All backlist available in ebook. Don't miss any of our special offers. Write to us at the following address for information on our newest releases.

Harlequin Reader Service
U.S.: 3010 Walden Ave., P.O. Box 1325, Buffalo, NY 14269
Canadian: P.O. Box 609, Fort Erie, Ont. L2A 5X3

CAST OF CHARACTERS

Danae LeBeau—The youngest LeBeau sister had the roughest childhood of the three girls, and it left her with a strong distrust of people and an attitude that anything life handed her, she would handle on her own. But with her life on the line, she has to trust someone, or risk dying alone.

Zach Sargent—The construction company owner was looking for answers surrounding his father's death and was certain they were contained on the LeBeau estate, where he'd gained a job as a contractor. He thought he'd have full access to the mansion, find the information he needed and leave, but the cagey LeBeau heiress kept him under her watchful eye. Could he convince her to trust him long enough to get the answers he needed?

Jack Granger—The disgruntled cook was mad enough that he didn't inherit from the LeBeau estate when the girls' stepfather died. He's even less thrilled that the woman who used to wait tables in the café turned out to be one of the heiresses. But was he angry enough to try kill her over it?

Bert Thibodeaux—The long-haul trucker had been promised an inheritance by the girls' stepfather, Trenton Purcell, but he got stiffed, just like the cook. He was no stranger to trouble with the law, but would he go as far as murder to take his revenge?

Johnny Miller—The local man had owned the café for decades and seemed to care about his patrons and the town. But was he another of the town's residents that Purcell had promised would inherit from the LeBeau estate?

Chapter One

The tortured soul wandered the mansion, calling for her children. Where had they gone? Why couldn't she hear their sweet voices? Why didn't their footsteps echo throughout the house?

Was it him? Had he done something to her babies?

The thought of it broke her heart and she screamed in anguish, vowing never to rest until her children were returned to her.

And until the man paid.

DANAE LEBEAU was running late, as usual, but today she had a good excuse. The local radio station had been abuzz since the wee hours of the morning, broadcasting information about the attack on Alaina LeBeau weeks before and the subsequent death of her attacker at the hands of the local sheriff. Until now, it had all been gossip and speculation, while everyone impatiently waited for the state police to clear those involved and declare it self-defense. Now it was the hottest bit of excitement the tiny bayou town of Calais had ever seen.

My sister could have died.

The thought ripped through her as she listened to the reporter relay the gruesome details of that horrible night at their mother's estate, the weight of the words crippling her. Her sister could have died, and Danae had never even told her they were related.

After their mother's death, the three sisters had been separated by their stepfather, Trenton Purcell, and shipped off to be raised by distant relatives. Danae was only two when it happened, not old enough to remember anything about her life in Calais. The only childhood she'd known was in California, but years ago, she'd started slowly making her way across the country to Louisiana. Even though she couldn't remember anything about her life in Calais, she'd always felt a tug—as if something was drawing her back to her birthplace.

Using an assumed name, she'd taken a job at the local café to try to find out information on her stepfather, who had lived as a recluse in her mother's family estate for over two decades. But she'd managed to find out very little about the man, given that most of the townspeople seemed to completely dislike him and were happy to see him disappear from society.

After her stepfather's death, Danae's sister Alaina showed up in Calais to meet the terms of their mother's will. According to the local gossip, each sister was required to live on the estate for a period of two weeks within one year after their stepfather's death. Once those stipulations were met, their mother's estate would pass to the sisters. It was shocking news to Danae, who'd always assumed their mother had left everything to their stepfather and that her ties to Calais had long since been severed.

Danae still remembered the day Alaina arrived in town. Through the storefront window of the café, she'd seen Alaina driving her SUV down Main Street. She'd dropped a whole stack of dishes and had her pay docked for the incident, but she hadn't been able to help it. The only thing Danae had from her past was an old photo of their mother. Alaina looked as if she'd stepped out of that photo, changed into current clothes and driven by.

When she met Alaina early one morning at the café, Danae wanted to tell her that they were sisters, but years of living on the street had taught her to always stand back and assess the situation. To always limit exposure of herself unless absolutely necessary. That level of caution had saved her life more than once, and just because she experienced a familial pull, she had no reason to sacrifice something that had always worked for her.

But now, she wondered if she should reveal herself. From the local talk, she had a good idea about the terms of the will and knew that if she wanted to take part, she'd have to come forward. The distant cousin who had taken her in when her mother died had passed away long ago, a liquor bottle clenched in her leathered hand, and Danae had never gotten close enough to anyone to make lasting friendships. If anyone tried to find her, the trail stopped cold in California.

After Danae met Alaina and got a good feeling about her as a person, she'd been tempted to talk to the estate attorney, but she'd still held back. What if their middle sister couldn't be located, either? Her understanding was that all three sisters had to meet the requirements of the will in order for any of them to inherit. If the last sister couldn't be located or didn't agree to the terms, then Danae would have exposed herself for no viable reason, and at a time when she didn't feel comfortable doing so.

But the attack on Alaina had her rethinking everything. What if her sister had died and she'd never gotten the chance to tell her who she was?

She could have missed one of her only opportunities to have a real family.

As she grabbed her car keys, she glanced at her watch and cursed. She even had the advantage of working second shift that morning, but she wasn't going to make the later work time, either. Johnny, the café owner, was going to kill her for being so late. Likely, everyone in Calais would wander through the café this morning to gossip about the news report. Nothing this big had ever happened in the sleepy bayou town. It was going to be the talk for quite a while.

She flung open the front door of her rented cabin, ready to break some major speeding laws on the winding country roads, but stopped short at the sight of the plain white envelope that lay on the welcome mat.

Such a common, nonthreatening item shouldn't have set off the wave of anxiety that flooded through her, but she immediately knew something was off. She hadn't let her guard down long enough to make close friends, and even if she had, they would hardly drive ten miles into the swamp to leave an envelope at her doorstep.

Her hands shook as she reached for the envelope, and as soon as her fingers closed around it, she set off at a run for her car. Whoever had left the envelope might be watching, lurking somewhere in the swamp that enclosed the tiny cabin and blocked it off from the rest of the world.

She jumped into her ancient sedan, started it and threw it into Drive, tearing out of the dirt driveway before she'd even managed to close the car door. She pressed the accelerator just beyond the limits of safety, and her fingers ached from clenching the steering wheel as the old car skidded in the gravel. The narrow road seemed to stretch on forever, but finally, she reached the intersection for the paved road that led into Calais.

She pulled to a stop and looked over at the envelope that she'd tossed onto the passenger's seat. Habit had her checking her rearview mirror, but no one was visible behind her. She glanced back at the passenger's seat where the envelope lay, seemingly taunting her to open it. Lifting one hand, she bit her lower lip, then hesitated.

What are you—a coward?

Unable to stand it any longer, she grabbed the envelope and tore it open. A single scrap of paper containing only one sentence fell out into her hand.

I know who you are.

She sucked in a breath so hard her chest ached. All her careful planning and secrecy had been for naught. Someone had figured out her secret. But why did they leave this message? What were they hoping to accomplish by doing so? Being Ophelia LeBeau's daughter wasn't a crime, and Danae had no reason other than an overzealous sense of self-protection for hiding her true identity.

Someone must be trying to scare her. But to what end?

She shoved the paper into her purse and continued her drive to town. She'd stop at the café first and let Johnny know she had to take a bit more time that morning. He wouldn't be happy and may even fire her, but that couldn't be helped. Danae had the sudden overwhelming feeling that she had to find William Duhon, the estate attorney, and reveal her true identity.

Whatever someone hoped to accomplish with the note, she was going to cut them off at the pass.

DANAE SPOTTED ALAINA'S SUV in front of the attorney's office and felt another bout of panic. Then logic took over and she decided it was a good thing. Might as well kill two birds with one stone. She hurried into the office and told a rather grim-looking woman at the front desk that she wished to speak to Mr. Duhon.

The grim woman frowned, which surprised

Danae a bit, as she'd thought the woman was already frowning before.

"Do you have an appointment?" Grim asked.

"You know that I don't," Danae replied, trying to keep her voice level. After all, this woman and everyone else knew her as Connie from the café, and probably couldn't imagine why she'd need to speak to William.

"I can make you an appointment for later this week."

"Is he talking to Alaina?"

"Mr. Duhon's clients are all afforded the privacy they deserve—"

Danae waved a hand at the woman to cut her off.

"Never mind," she said as she walked past the desk and pushed open the door to the attorney's office.

Alaina jumped around in her seat when Danae flung open the door, and the attorney jumped up from his chair, uncertain and clearly uncomfortable with the interruption.

"You can't go in there," Grim admonished behind her.

"I'm Danae LeBeau," she said before she could change her mind.

Chapter Two

Alaina and William stared at her, their expressions a mixture of disbelief and surprise. She'd expected as much. Connie Smith, café waitress, had served them both breakfast on many occasions. She'd never provided her real name to anyone in Calais before now. And as her looks were a perfect blend of both parents, she didn't favor either enough to draw suspicion.

"I have documentation," she said and pulled some faded, worn papers from her purse. "A birth certificate and a driver's license with my real name—I'd appreciate it if you don't ask where I got the one I've been using."

She stood there, holding the documents, with both William and Alaina staring at her in shock. Finally, Alaina rose from her chair and walked the couple of steps to stand in front of her.

"Danae?" Alaina said, her voice wavering. "You were just a toddler… You had on a new dress that day—"

"Yellow with white roses," Danae interrupted.

Alaina's eyes filled with tears. "Yes." She threw her arms around Danae and squeezed her tightly. "I never thought… When I came here, I didn't know what would happen."

Danae struggled to maintain her composure. "I didn't know, either."

"Why didn't you tell me when I first arrived?"

"We're fine, Ms. Morgan," William's voice sounded behind them.

Danae released Alaina and glanced back in time to see Secretary Grim pull the door closed, her frown still fixed in place. Alaina smiled at her and wiped her cheeks with the back of her hand.

"I…uh…" Danae struggled to find a way to explain. "I don't really know why I came to Calais, or even to Louisiana. I mean, I guess I thought I could talk to our stepfather and maybe find out something—anything—about my past, maybe find you and Joelle. But I never got the chance and then he died."

Danae sniffed and willed the tears that were building to stay in place. Now was not the time to go soft. "I don't really remember. I don't remember anything, and I kept thinking that it was important. That my life here mattered and I needed to know. I know it sounds silly…"

Alaina squeezed her arm. "No. It doesn't sound silly at all. Not to me."

Danae could tell by the way Alaina said it that she meant what she said. She wasn't just being nice. She understood, as only the three sisters could possibly understand. A wave of relief passed over her, and the tug at her heart, the one she'd felt for Alaina the first time she saw her, grew stronger.

"I'm sure you've heard about how our stepfather lived," Danae continued. "I never even saw him. Then he died and you turned up."

Alaina smiled. "I felt a connection to you when we first met that I didn't understand. I slipped so easily into conversation with you, which is rare. Maybe somewhere deep down, I knew."

Danae sniffed and her eyes misted up a bit. "I wanted to say something when you arrived, but what would people think—my working here with an assumed name and all?"

She looked over at the attorney. "I swear I didn't know about the inheritance when I came to Calais."

The attorney waved a hand at the chairs in front of his desk, encouraging them to sit. "Please don't trouble yourself with those kinds of thoughts, Ms. LeBeau. You couldn't have been aware of the conditions of your mother's will. Ophelia was a very private person, and your stepfather wasn't about to tell anyone that he wasn't really the wealthy man he seemed."

As Danae slid into the chair next to Alaina, she felt some of the tension lessen in her shoulders and back. "But I still came here under false pretenses."

"No," Alaina said. "You came here looking for answers and didn't want everyone to know that evil old man was your stepfather. I hardly think anyone will fault you for your feelings."

The attorney nodded. "Your sister is correct. While some of the more dramatic of Calais's residents may find some fun in theorizing as to your hidden identity, those who partake in logical thinking will not so much as raise an eyebrow at your choices. In fact, most would assume you wise."

Danae smiled. "You're very refreshing, Mr. Duhon."

"Isn't he the best?" Alaina beamed. "Until I met him, I had no idea attorneys could be competent, nice and have a personality. I'd thought I was the only one."

"Please call me William," he said, a slight blush creeping up his neck. "Well, ladies, we have a lot to discuss, but I can cover the basics of the inheritance now and we can meet at a later date to discuss the rest."

Danae nodded. "I know I have to live on the property for two weeks and that Sheriff Trahan will verify my residency every day. At least, that's what the café gossip is."

"This time, the café gossip is correct. That was one of the things Alaina and I were discussing, among everything else."

"Why? Have the requirements changed?"

"No, but the storm last week did a lot of damage. Much of the house no longer has power, and the heating system has failed completely. Essentially, the house has gone from barely habitable to not habitable in a matter of days."

Danae pulled at a loose thread on the chair cushion. "So what do we do?" The thought of living in that big, scary house with limited power wasn't anywhere on her bucket list.

William frowned. "That is a fine question. I have already hired someone to begin the repairs, but the work could take a while to complete. I assume you'd like to get this over with."

Danae nodded.

He tapped his pen on the desk then jumped up with more speed than Danae would have thought possible for a man his age. He pulled open a drawer in the filing cabinet behind him and removed a thick folder.

He slid back into his chair and flipped through the pages, scanning and frowning as he went. Danae looked over at Alaina, but she just shrugged. Finally, he closed the document and beamed across the desk at them.

"You're renting the cabin off Bayou Glen Drive, right?" William asked.

"Yes," Danae replied, "but I don't see—"

"That cabin is part of the estate," William said. "The inheritance documents don't specify that you must occupy the main house, so I'm to assume that if you wanted to pitch a tent somewhere on estate acreage, that would also qualify. But in your case, you merely have to remain where you are for at least another two weeks, subject to monitoring and verification by our friend the sheriff."

"Oh!" Danae exclaimed. "Well, that's great."

Alaina clapped her hands. "I told you William is the best."

The ring of a cell phone interrupted their celebration. Alaina pulled her phone out of her purse and glanced at the display.

"I'm sorry," Alaina said. "I have to take this."

Alaina said very little but Danae could tell by the tone of her voice that something was wrong. Her sister frowned as she slipped the phone back into her purse.

"Is everything okay?" Danae asked.

"No. My mother—the one who raised me— fell yesterday and broke her leg. My father died a couple years back, and my stepbrother and stepsister both work full-time and can't afford to take off. They know I resigned from the firm and asked if I can stay with her for a week or so until the home health nurse is available."

Disappointment rolled over Danae and she tried to fight it down. Of course Alaina had to go help the woman who'd raised her, but she'd been hoping for long hours to catch up with her sister—to pick her memory for glimpses of their life before their mother died. Surely Alaina, the oldest of the sisters, had memories of their childhood.

Alaina put her hand on Danae's arm. "I'm so sorry to have to leave right now."

"Don't be silly," Danae said. "We have plenty of time. I'm not going anywhere, not even after my two weeks are up."

Alaina leaned over and hugged her before rising from her chair. "I need to book a flight and pack a bag. You gave me your cell-phone number weeks ago, so I'll call you as soon as I get a chance and you'll have mine. I think there's a midmorning flight to Boston that I may be able to catch if I hurry."

Alaina hurried around the desk to plant a kiss on a blushing William's cheek, then rushed out of the office, closing the door behind her.

William watched Alaina, smiling, then looked

at Danae after she'd gone. "She's quite a woman, your sister. I think you two are going to get along very well."

"I've liked her since the moment I met her. That's a real relief for me. That and the fact that she wasn't disappointed that I'm her sister."

"Why would she be?"

"I don't know—I mean, she's this big-shot attorney and I'm just a café waitress. We're hardly in the same realm."

"You had two very different upbringings after you were stripped from your home." He gave her a kindly look. "In my attempts to locate you, I learned some about your life in California. You've done well for yourself, Danae. Please don't ever doubt that."

She sniffed at the unexpected kindness. "Thanks."

A movie reel of where she'd come from up to where she was now flashed through her mind, and she realized that right now was the turning point—the time where she could choose to make everything in her life different or simply fade away into obscurity again. It was exhilarating and frightening at the same time.

"I can still have access to the house, right?" she asked.

"Yes, of course. It is—or will be—your property, after all. Is there anything in particular you wanted to do? Alaina made quite a dent in remodeling and cleaning. Her work in the kitchen transformed the room."

She smiled. "I'm sure cleaning is something I could handle, but what I really want is the ability to go through the papers and pictures—see if I can find stuff about our past with our mother. I was so young…"

"And you want to remember." William sighed. "It makes me so sad that you girls grew up without your mother. Ophelia was such a wonderful woman and her delight in you girls was apparent. Her death was a loss to the entire community but was devastating for you girls."

He removed his glasses and rubbed them with a cleaning cloth on his desk, and Danae could tell he still felt her mother's death. It made her both happy and sad that her mother was such a wonderful person she'd left such an impression, but then died without living her life to the fullest.

William slipped his glasses back on and cleared his throat. "It so happens that I need someone to go through the documents in the house. I haven't been able to find anyone willing to do the work at the house, so I was going to have everything boxed up and shipped to an analyst in New Orleans. But if you're willing to do the work, I'd be happy to pay you, instead of removing the documents."

"What are you looking for?"

"Inventory lists, receipts—anything that gives me the ability to construct a list of property. I need to have it evaluated for tax purposes and such. So much is stuffed in the attic, closets and heaven only knows where else that it would take years to uncover it all. I hoped that the most valuable of objects would be contained on an asset listing or that the receipts would be filed with important household documents. Then I could valuate those items, assuming we locate them, and assign a base value to everything else."

Danae could only imagine the mess that must be contained inside the massive old mansion. William definitely had his work cut out for him.

"I know you have your job at the café," William continued, "so please don't feel you have to accept my offer, but I wouldn't feel right if I didn't tell you the rate for the work is twenty-five dollars an hour."

"Seriously?"

"It's boring and dirty work, but requires concentration and attention to detail. The rate is standard for this sort of thing."

Danae ran a mental budget through her head. The rate was considerably more than she made at the café, but once the job was over, what would she do? If she quit now, it would be unlikely that she could get the job back. The waitress she'd replaced six months ago had moved off to New Orleans with her boyfriend, but that relationship had ended and she was back in Calais and hoping for her old job back.

"I anticipate the work will take several months," William said and Danae wondered if he could read her mind. "And during your two-week inheritance stint, you won't be required to pay rent. The estate can hardly charge you for meeting the terms of the will, but the remainder of the lease has to stay in effect."

In several months, she could easily save enough money to cover herself for more than a year. She had no debt and knew how to live on next to nothing. And maybe, if the job lasted long enough, she'd make enough to invest in the future she really wanted—to become a chef. Twenty-five an hour would go a good ways toward paying for culinary school in New Orleans.

"I think I'll take that job," she said.

William beamed. "Good. I'll have my secretary draw up the paperwork."

"Great," she said, hoping she wasn't making a mistake.

"You know, I haven't located Joelle yet, but

I have a solid lead and expect to find your sister before month's end. I have no doubt I can convince her to take part in the inheritance requirements."

Danae shook her head. "What if she's got a family, a job…things she can't just up and leave?"

"Yes, all those things matter, but the reality is, with you and Alaina meeting the requirements, Joelle has no risk. Taking those two weeks out of her life will leave all three of you so wealthy that you'll never have to work again unless you choose to."

Danae sucked in a breath. "I didn't… I had no idea."

"Why would you? The estate looks like it needs a bulldozer rather than a cleaning, but the reality is your mother was an incredibly wealthy woman, and even your stepfather couldn't manage to put a dent in her accumulated fortune."

"So once Joelle finishes her two weeks, I…"

"Have the entire world at your fingertips. Whatever you desire for a future, you'll have the means to pursue it." He smiled. "Unless, of course, serving coffee and incredible pie to aging attorneys and disgruntled sheriffs is where your dreams lie."

She laughed. "You make it sound so tempting."

"Yes, well, as much as I'd love to see that

beautiful smile at Johnny's Café, I prefer for you to have what you want most. It may take a while," he warned, "to locate Joelle, finish up her term and then push the entire mess through Louisiana's often frustrating legal system. But it shouldn't take more than eighteen months, even if Joelle doesn't fulfill her time right until the end of the year allotted."

"Eighteen months," Danae repeated, trying to wrap her mind around everything the attorney had told her. She'd settled in Calais hoping to find out something about her past, with the ultimate dream of locating her sisters. Her mother's will had come as a huge surprise to her and everyone else in Calais, but the knowledge that her mother's fortune remained intact astounded her.

Even in her wildest dreams—even after hearing about her mother's will—she'd never imagined much would come of it. Rather, she'd thought they would inherit a run-down monstrosity of a house that would be fraught with issues and impossible to sell. But this…this was something out of a fairy tale.

William opened his desk drawer and pulled out a huge black key. "This is the key to the front door," he said as he pushed it across the desk to her. "It's an old locking system, but it's well-oiled. You shouldn't have any problems with access."

She picked up the key, feeling the weight of the old iron in her hand, and thought about everything that single object represented. It was quite literally going to unlock the rest of her life.

"There is one other thing," William said.

A sliver of uncertainty ran through her at the apprehension she detected in the attorney's voice. "Yes?"

"I'm sure you heard that Amos broke his foot and will be staying with his niece here in town."

Danae nodded. Amos was the estate's caretaker and no less than eighty years old, hence the general run-down state of the house and grounds. Her stepfather had refused to hire additional help, and the aging caretaker had been unable to maintain it all himself.

"I'd mentioned before that I've hired a contractor to address the problems at the house," William continued. "He will arrive today and will stay in Amos's cabin. His name is Zach Sargent. He'll need daily access to the house, but I'm going to leave it up to you whether or not you provide him with a key, as you'll also be working inside. If you're uncomfortable with anyone else besides myself, Alaina and the sheriff having free access, I can arrange for someone to let him in daily."

Her gut clenched a little at the thought of a strange man who could enter the house at any time. "Actually, I can let him in and out myself," she said. "I'm an early riser and plan on spending full-time hours working on the files."

William nodded and pulled another key from his drawer. "This is a key to the caretaker's cabin," he said as he pushed it across the desk to her. "I had it stocked with basic supplies yesterday, and I've already made arrangements with the general store for any supplies or tools he needs."

"Great." At least she didn't have to manage the supplies end of things.

"The road—not much more than a path, really—to the caretaker's cabin is at the north end of the main house's driveway. The path leads straight to the cabin, so there's no chance of his getting lost. Just point him in the right direction. I'm sure he can take it from there."

Danae nodded. "You said he'll arrive today?"

"Probably later this afternoon."

"That's good," she said as she rose, the note she'd found on her doorstep weighing heavily on her. But despite her genuine fondness for the attorney, something prevented her from mentioning the incident to him.

"I better run," she said, before she changed her mind and blurted out everything about the note. "I need to square things away with Johnny at the café. How do I handle the work for you?"

William rose from his chair. "Start going through the paperwork—your stepfather's office is the logical choice to begin. Put everything you think relevant for my purposes in a box and keep a log of your time. I'll check in periodically and we'll cut you a check every Friday, if that is all right by you. Don't worry about the hours. The estate is happy to pay for whatever you're willing to work."

"That's great." She extended her hand and clasped his. "Thank you...for everything."

William gave her hand a squeeze. "It's been my pleasure."

She smiled and walked out of his office, giving Secretary Grim a nod on her way through the lobby. After she'd slid into her car, she clenched the steering wheel with both hands, trying to process everything that had happened that morning, but her whirling mind couldn't put it all into neat little boxes.

She'd almost slipped up in there—almost broken down and given William and Alaina more information than she would have normally. It was so unexpected for her to feel that comfortable with other people that she was surprised at herself. Granted, her sister and William seemed to be perfectly nice and straightforward, but her natural distrust of everyone had saved her more times than she could recall. Now was not the time to abandon a way of life that had worked well for her. At least, not until she knew more about Alaina and William.

She blew out a breath and backed her car out of the parking space. It didn't matter that she hadn't told William about the note she'd found that morning. Someone had made a lucky guess and hoped to scare her away or create drama for her. Now that she'd announced herself and stolen their thunder, likely, they'd go away.

At least, that was what she was going to keep telling herself.

Chapter Three

It was almost three o'clock when Zach Sargent pulled into the tiny bayou town of Calais. He shook his head, still not believing his luck. Landing the repair job at the LeBeau estate was an opportunity he'd never even imagined existed, much less that he'd be the one to snag it.

Granted, most men would choose higher-paying construction jobs near the New Orleans nightlife before they'd sequester themselves deep in the swamps of Mystere Parish, but Zach wasn't most men. Far more was at stake than a paycheck and a good time.

Somewhere inside the crumbling walls of the LeBeau estate, he hoped to find the answers to the questions his dad had left him with. Zach knew it was possible that his dad's words had only been the ramblings of a man drugged up and near death, but something in his dad's voice troubled him to the point that he needed to find answers.

He'd thought the words would fade after his burial, but they haunted Zach in his dreams and nagged at him while he was awake. Finally, he'd given up fighting it and started a thorough search of his dad's records from the time his dad had spoken of. It had only taken a couple of days to come across the entry in his checkbook that had made Zach's breath catch in his throat. A twenty-thousand-dollar deposit with no explanation noted.

What had his dad done?

What had he regretted so much that he'd laid on his son a garbled confession of some wrongdoing?

Zach had spent many hours since discovering the unexplained deposit trying to imagine what his dad's secret could be. His father had been an honorable man, a good man, raising Zach alone after his mother passed when he was only eight. Zach simply couldn't wrap his mind around his dad doing something so horrible that he felt he had to make it right before he died.

If only he'd spoken to Zach before that last stroke, before his speech was so impaired and before he was so drugged that he couldn't maintain a semblance of coherence. But all of that was wishful thinking and a waste of time.

His dad had said only one name during his ramblings—Ophelia LeBeau.

Somewhere in that house were the answers Zach sought. He had to believe that. It was the only thing that allowed him to sleep at night. And now he had the opportunity to find out for himself.

When he reached the second crossroads outside of Calais, he checked the map the estate attorney had provided and turned to the right. His truck bumped on the sad excuse for a road, and the farther he drove, the denser the trees and foliage became. If he hadn't known it was only noon, he'd have thought it was dusk. The faintest streams of sunlight managed to peek through the top layers of the cypress trees, but by the time that light penetrated the thick moss clinging to the tree branches, it was filtered to only a dim glow.

If he'd tried, he couldn't have come farther from his Bourbon Street flat than this expanse of seemingly never-ending swamp. He'd expected remote, but he hadn't expected to feel so enclosed, so claustrophobic. After all, he lived in an eight-hundred-square-foot flat. Miles of dirt and water should make him feel less confined, not more so.

He shook his head, clearing his mind of fanciful thoughts that had no place there, and ran through his plan once he'd gained access to the house and the records. With any luck, everything would be well organized and he'd find his answer quickly. Honor and loyalty would force him to complete the work needed on the house, even if he got his answer the first day, but the work would be easier and go more quickly without the distraction of the unanswered question hanging over his head.

His truck dipped into a large pothole and he cursed as he gripped the steering wheel more firmly, trying to maintain control of the vehicle as it lurched sideways. If he had to replace anything in the house that was breakable, he'd have to creep down this road to keep from destroying things before he even got them there.

Finally, when he thought he'd driven straight across the United States to Canada, he turned a final corner, and the house loomed before him. Involuntarily, he lifted his foot from the gas, and the truck rolled almost to a stop as he stared at the imposing structure.

The architect in him formed an immediate appreciation for the bold lines and refined features of the mansion. The part of him dedicated to B horror movies was certain he'd driven straight into a midnight feature.

It was horrifying and seductive, all at the same time.

He inched the truck around the decrepit stone driveway and parked behind an ancient sedan.

The attorney's car, he thought as he exited the truck and made his way to the massive double doors. He scanned the door frame for a bell, but didn't see anything resembling such a device, so he rapped on the solid wood door.

Seconds later, the door flew open and he found himself staring at someone who clearly was not the aging male attorney he'd spoken to on the phone.

The girl in front of him was small but toned, with short black hair and amber eyes that were narrowed on him. It took him a couple of seconds to realize that despite her youthful appearance, she was more woman than girl, and a bit of relief coursed through him because the male part of him had been instantly appreciative of her trim body and chiseled facial features.

The woman's shrewd eyes looked him up and down and glanced at his vehicle, quickly making an assessment, but when he expected her to speak, she just stared directly at him, her eyes locked on his, unwavering.

"I'm Zach Sargent," he said finally, extending his hand. "I'm the contractor William Duhon hired to make the repairs to the house."

The woman hesitated a second before briefly clasping his hand, then releasing it. "I'm Danae LeBeau," she said.

Zach felt his pulse quicken. Could this woman

be Ophelia LeBeau's daughter? William had mentioned that one of the heiresses had been living in the house, but the name Danae didn't ring any bells.

She stepped back and opened the door for him to enter. "I have the key to the caretaker's cottage in the kitchen."

Zach stepped inside and did a double take at the gloomy interior, layered with dust and sadly lacking in basic maintenance and care. The attorney had said the property needed a lot of work, but Zach thought it had been occupied until recently. He was somewhat shocked that a person would choose to live like this.

"You coming?" Danae asked, her eyebrows arched.

Before he could reply, she continued down a wide hallway to the left of the entry. He blew out a breath and followed her down the hall, then drew up short in the kitchen. The room was a refreshing change from the entry. Stone countertops and floors gleamed, the cabinets and dining table were polished to a high sheen and a new coat of paint covered the walls.

"Is something wrong?"

"What…? No," he replied, realizing he'd been casing the room like an eager real-estate agent or petty thief. "Sorry, I was just taking in the contrast between this room and the entry."

Danae nodded. "My sister started cleaning and remodeling here a couple of weeks ago, but hasn't had time to get much more done."

Zach frowned. "I don't understand. William said the house had been occupied until recently."

"By our stepfather. My sisters and I haven't been allowed to set foot here since we were sent away as children...when our mother died."

Her jaw flexed when she delivered that information, and some of the bitter edge the heiress displayed began to make sense. "I'm sorry. I didn't mean to bring up a sensitive subject."

"You're not the first. Won't be the last." She pulled a key out of her purse and placed it on the end of the counter. "That's the key to the caretaker's cabin. The path to the cabin is at the north end of the main driveway. William had it stocked with basic living supplies, but he has you set up with the general store to handle anything beyond that."

He nodded. "Great. And what about a key to the main house?"

She stiffened and shook her head. "The house isn't habitable in the shape it's in, but I'm going to be working here, as well. I'll let you in every morning and lock up at night."

Zach struggled to maintain his aggravation, but knew if he made a big deal out of having free access to the house, she may start to wonder. Still, being under constant scrutiny wasn't going to get him what he'd come for. He had to find an angle that worked.

"Are you sure?" he asked, trying to sound casual. "I prefer to start early."

She'd been gazing out the back window, but when he delivered his last sentence, she looked directly at him—pinned him with those dark eyes—and he got the impression she wasn't buying what he'd said. Not completely.

"I've worked in cafés and bars for years. I'm used to getting up early and finishing up late, and as I have no other personal business in this town except the estate, your work won't interfere with my schedule."

"Okay, then. I guess I'll see you tomorrow morning at seven. If that's all right?"

"No problem at all."

"Have a good evening," he said and started down the hall to the front entry. Zach knew when he'd lost the battle. As much as he didn't need the interference, he'd have to play things Danae's way.

At least until he could find a way around her.

Chapter Four

Danae peered out a tiny crack in the front door, watching Zach drive away. He hadn't been at all what she'd expected when William had told her he'd hired a contractor. She'd thought someone older, someone not as adept at repair as they used to be, would be the only person interested in a job out in the middle of the swamp. The young, gorgeous man who'd just left was the absolute last person she'd thought would be interested in a job in a town like Calais.

With his light brown hair, piercing green eyes and stellar body, Zach belonged in the heart of New Orleans, charming all the ladies who came downtown looking for a good time. He certainly didn't fit Calais and the LeBeau estate.

Frowning, she pushed the heavy wooden door shut, unable to shake the feeling that something about the sexy contractor didn't add up. Briefly, it crossed her mind that he was running from something, but she dismissed the thought as soon as it came. He didn't have that look of flight, and she knew that look well. She'd worn it several times herself and seen it in many others.

Finally, she sighed. Likely, it was something simple and embarrassing. If bartending had taught her anything, it was that most people had some secret that they kept locked away from others. The secret wasn't often earth-shattering, but simply something the person felt would change others' opinions of them. Maybe Zach had such a secret—like a gambling or drinking problem. Something that had given him a bad reputation with construction companies in New Orleans.

She shook her head to clear her thoughts of Zach and the many different things he could be hiding and tried to focus on what she wanted to tackle next. She'd arrived at the house only twenty minutes before noon, and aside from talking to Zach, she'd spent the rest of the time doing a run-through of the downstairs rooms, checking windows and exterior doors to ensure no unwanted guests could enter.

By the time she had finished her review of the downstairs, she expected Zach to arrive at any moment and had been unwilling to start poking around upstairs. She preferred instead to get her meeting with the contractor out of the way and delve more into her past when she was alone again with the memories that she couldn't seem to access.

She had just decided to head upstairs and get a feel for the rooms there when her cell phone rang. She checked the display and frowned. It wasn't a number she recognized, but it definitely wasn't in Louisiana.

She answered and was happy to hear Alaina's voice.

"I'm so sorry," Alaina said. "I meant to call earlier, but I didn't charge my cell before leaving, so it's dead as a doornail. This is the first opportunity I've had to break away from the family and call you. I hope you didn't think I'd forgotten."

"No, of course not. How is your...er, mother?"

Even though she didn't really know Alaina at all, it still felt strange calling another woman her sister's mother. She wondered how it felt for Alaina.

"She's doing fine, considering. My brother has a service lined up for home care until she can get around again, but they are on another job at the moment and not expected to free up for another week at least."

A twinge of something—sadness...jealousy—passed through Danae when Alaina said *my brother* but she pushed it aside. Their stepfather hadn't given any of the girls a choice when he'd sent them away. Alaina couldn't help it if she'd gotten a decent family, while Danae had gotten an addict. That was simply the luck of the draw.

"I'm glad she's okay," Danae said.

"Me, too, but the timing couldn't be worse. I'm so sorry I had to dash out this morning like I did. I have a million things to talk to you about. If I started now, I probably couldn't finish by next year."

Danae smiled. "I know."

"But first things first—I am so glad you don't have to stay in that house. When I thought about you staying there, my chest hurt so bad I felt like it was in a vise."

"I'm at the house now. It's not exactly a welcoming sort of place."

"No, but it's more than that. It's…I don't know… Oh, I'll just say it. I think there's something wrong in that house. I know you don't really know me, but I promise you, I'm not a fanciful sort of person. And given my profession, my senses are better honed than many. I know something's off. I can feel it in every inch of my body."

Danae tensed at her sister's description. It was the same way she'd felt since she'd walked into the house.

Alaina sighed. "I bet I sound like a crazy woman."

"I almost wish you did, but you're not crazy. I feel it, too. And let's just say my survival skills are as finely tuned as your ability to recognize when things don't add up. They're firing on all eight cylinders here. But I have no idea why."

"I don't, either, and that's what concerns me the most. I'm not trying to tell you what to do, but I wish you wouldn't go there at all."

"William has hired me to go through the paperwork and attempt an inventory of the valuables, so I don't have a choice, and I really want to do the work. I want to discover things about our past. Things I'll probably never remember."

Alaina was quiet for several seconds, then finally she said, "I tried to find you—you and Joelle. I started writing letters to Purcell when I was in high school, asking him to tell me how to find you. I even tried sending him a letter on the law firm's letterhead when I got to Baton Rouge."

"But he never answered," Danae finished. "He wouldn't have. I spent months looking for that opening where I could get to him, but there wasn't one. He was a mentally disturbed old man who only cared about himself. He never would have helped any of us."

"You're probably right. I understand why you want to try to find some of the things that were torn away from you, but I still don't like the idea of you being in that house alone. Can you at least work at your cabin until I return?"

Danae felt a tickle of warmth run through her. The concern in Alaina's voice was so sincere and passionate—something she'd never experienced until now. It was everything she'd ever wanted and something she'd never counted on getting.

"When we get off the phone, I'll grab some files and take them home with me today. The contractor starts tomorrow, so I won't be alone. He's young and looks like he'd be good in a fight."

"Well, I guess that's all right."

Alaina didn't sound the least bit convinced, but Danae couldn't exactly fault her when she wasn't convinced herself.

"Purcell's office is upstairs at the end of the right hallway," Alaina said. "The room I stayed in—our childhood room—is at the end of the left hallway, right over the kitchen. The power is out in the office area of the house, so it will be dark. There're some flashlights and a lantern in the laundry-room cabinet."

"Thanks. That helps a lot," Danae replied as she committed all the information to memory.

"Danae," Alaina said, "I know this is going to sound completely odd, but I have to ask you something."

"Okay."

"Do you believe in ghosts?"

Danae's breath caught in her throat. Of all the things she'd thought Alaina might ask, that hadn't been anywhere on the list.

Before she could formulate a reply, she heard background noise on Alaina's end.

"I'm so sorry," Alaina said, "but I'm going to have to go. I'll call you again as soon as I get a chance."

Alaina disconnected and Danae set the phone back on the counter. Ghosts? Sure, all kinds of rumors about the house and its other-than-earthly inhabitants wafted about the Calais locales, but it was the sort of thing she'd expect in a small town with a run-down, isolated house. It was not the kind of thing a reputable, hard-nosed attorney would normally come up with.

It made Danae wonder exactly how much she didn't know about the night Alaina was attacked.

She leaned back against the counter and blew out a breath. All the work she'd done to simplify her life. No strings, no baggage—at least not the

physical kind. She'd even come to Calais with
an assumed identity simply to avoid the looks
and questions she was sure would come. And in
less than a day, her life had become more complicated than it had ever been.

This is what you wanted.

And that was what she needed to keep reminding herself. In the past, she'd kept her life
simple by avoiding anything beyond surface-
level relationships, but she'd come to Calais
to find her family. She couldn't have it both
ways. If she wanted a family, she had to drop
her guard, at least where her sisters were concerned.

She pushed herself off the counter and headed
upstairs for the first time. She paused on the
landing, trying to remember what Alaina had
told her about the layout. Right was Purcell's office. Left was the girls' room—the room Alaina
had been staying in when she was attacked.

Danae took one step in that direction, then
froze. Was she ready to see the place where
she'd spent her very limited childhood in Calais? If she had no memory of that room, then
the chances of her remembering anything were
so minuscule as to not exist. Not that she'd had
any concrete expectation of remembering things
she'd last seen at two years old, but she'd hoped

for an emotional tug—something that let her know a piece of this place was part of her.

Something that let her know where she fit.

Abruptly, she turned and headed in the opposite direction, to her stepfather's office.

Coward.

Ignoring the voice in her head, she increased her pace. Plenty of time existed for her to see her childhood bedroom, she argued. She had no reason to try to force it all into one afternoon. When she was comfortable with the house, she'd go to the room.

Or when she was ready for the disappointment.

Sighing, she pushed open the last door in the hallway and reached inside for a light switch, hoping the power had been miraculously restored. No such luck. She stepped inside the room and flicked the switch up and down to no avail. It figured. First thing tomorrow, she'd ask Zach to look at the electrical problems, starting with this room.

The light from the balcony was the only source of illumination in the office. The lack of windows and cherrywood bookcases that lined every wall made it so dark it was impossible to see more than the dim outline of office furniture. She cursed under her breath at her lapse of logical judgment. Alaina had told her about the flashlights in the laundry room. She should have grabbed one before coming up here.

She backed out of the room, but as she started to turn, she caught a glimpse of something out of the corner of her eye. She froze and stared into the darkness at the far end of the room, where she'd seen the flicker of movement. Nothing moved there now, but everything in Danae screamed at her that she was not alone in the house.

She whirled around and ran all the way downstairs and back into the kitchen, where she'd left her purse. It was still on the kitchen counter, and she snatched it up. From the inside pocket, she drew out the nine millimeter she was never without.

Let that be a lesson.

With the distraction of Zach Sargent, and her first visit to her childhood home, and her conversation with her sister, she'd forgotten to keep protection within arm's reach. Her sister's attacker was dead and gone, but more than one danger could exist.

Even in the same house.

Clenching the pistol, she eased down the hallway and across the entry to the laundry room. Two flashlights and a lantern were located right where Alaina had said they'd be. She clicked on a flashlight to make sure it worked, then headed back upstairs to the office.

She crept down the hallway toward the office and paused just before the doorway, listening for any sound of movement inside. Not even a breath of air swept by, so she stepped into the doorway and turned on the flashlight, shining it in the corner where she'd seen the movement.

The corner was empty, but the last bookcase appeared to have an odd angle to it—one that didn't fit with the other wall. Clenching the flashlight in one hand and her pistol in the other, she stepped across the room to the back wall, where she was surprised to find a narrow opening at the back of the wall. When looking into the room from the doorway, the opening was almost hidden by the bookcase.

The room was pitch-black, and for a moment, she wished she'd brought the lantern as well as the flashlight. Shining the flashlight across the room, she realized this must have been her stepfather's bedroom. The office entrance was the last doorway in the hallway, so at some point, her bizarre stepfather must have closed off the main entrance to the bedroom, leaving the office as the only access to his private quarters.

Just how crazy was he?

At the first opportunity, that was a question she'd explore with William, and perhaps pay a visit to Amos, the caretaker, while he was recovering at his niece's house. She stepped into the room and slowly cast the thin flashlight beam across the room, moving left to right. On the left, at the back of the room, she saw another door and the light fell across a claw-foot tub beyond it. Then she scanned over his bed, still made up with sheets, and paused at the nightstand, with its collection of pill bottles and a half-empty glass of water still standing next to them.

Clearly, Alaina hadn't spent much time, if any, in this room. Not that she blamed her. The room was unsettling. The air was stiller, as if she'd stepped into a vacuum, and not a single sound echoed through the exterior walls and into the bedroom.

Like a tomb.

The thought ripped through her, and despite the heat of early fall, she shivered. The thought was too accurate for comfort. Her stepfather had locked himself away from society, then practically barricaded himself in this room and died. It was something a sane person simply couldn't wrap their mind around.

She lifted the flashlight beam from the nightstand and continued along the back wall to the right, where she almost missed a wooden door, carved to match the paneling. Closet, maybe?

She didn't want to take another step into the room, but she would be working just outside this room and had to know that it was secure. Her heart pounded as she inched across the bedroom, feeling as if every step took her farther and farther away from safety. When she reached the door, she placed the flashlight on the nightstand, the light shining onto the ceiling and casting a dim glow around her.

She tightened her grip on the pistol and slowly turned the doorknob and eased the door open. As the light filtered into the opening, she frowned. The clothes she'd expected to see were nowhere in sight. Instead, a steep flight of stairs led down to the first floor.

A shock wave of fear ran through her and she released the doorknob and staggered back a couple of steps. During her tour of the first floor, she'd found the servants' stairwell close to the laundry room, but she'd assumed the entry would be off the hallway upstairs. She'd never considered that the stairs would lead straight into the master bedroom.

Someone could have been here.

She grabbed the flashlight and hurried out of the room and back downstairs, rushing across the entry to the back of the house, where she'd seen the exit for the servants' stairs. The door was closed, but before she could think about all the potential dangers, she yanked it open, pointing her pistol inside.

She hadn't realized she'd been holding her breath until it rushed out in a whoosh. *Get a grip,* she told herself as she pushed the door shut, noting that it didn't make a sound as it closed. If someone had passed this way earlier, she wouldn't have heard them exit. But the big question was, if someone had been in the house, where were they now?

The laundry room was at the end of the hallway, just a few feet beyond the servants' stairs. She hurried to the laundry room to check the back door. The knob turned easily in her hand, and she pushed the door open and looked out into the backyard that had been swallowed up by the swamp. Vines and moss clung to every branch of the cypress trees that loomed above, while moss and weeds choked out any remaining sign of lawn.

She stared at the tangle of foliage and decided it made her just as uneasy as the master bedroom. It wasn't just here, either. The swamp surrounding her cabin felt equally as ominous— as if it were a living entity and resented her trespass. For a girl who'd lived in some of the toughest neighborhoods across the country, it was unnerving to get such powerful feelings from a bunch of trees and brush.

She pushed the door shut and locked the dead bolt, her mind made up. Someone had been in the house. They'd stayed hidden upstairs while she was searching the first floor, then used her trip upstairs as an opportunity to slip out of the house unseen. They probably thought she'd dismiss the unlatched back door as an oversight, but they were wrong. Street-smart women like Danae didn't have "oversights" on things as important as exterior doors, and she was certain it was locked when she'd examined the first floor earlier.

In the past, when her safety had been threatened, she'd simply packed up and moved on. She'd had no roots and nothing of value to keep her tied to any one place, especially a dangerous one. But now she had something to lose. Something huge. Running was out of the question, so she hurried back to the kitchen and pulled out her cell phone.

For the first time in her life, she was calling the police.

Chapter Five

Zach paced the tiny caretaker's cottage, aggravated with almost everything. His original enthusiasm over scoring the LeBeau estate job was seriously compromised after meeting Danae Le-Beau. The heiress had enchanting features and a stellar body, but was prickly and suspicious and was already making a mess of his carefully laid plans.

How was he supposed to dig around in the house records with her looking over his shoulder? If she were going to be at the house every day alongside him, that didn't leave him any opportunity to snoop during that time. Now his only option was to find a way inside the house so that he could search for his answers at night.

Maybe he'd luck into a spare key lying around. If not, then he'd make sure to leave a window unlocked—a downstairs one with easy access, if such a thing existed. The swamp had almost swallowed the house, the brush and weeds pushing their way right up to the house walls.

He stopped pacing and ran one hand through his hair. What the hell was he supposed to do until tomorrow morning? Even if he could have distracted his overloaded mind with television, the caretaker didn't own a set. No television, no radio, not even a crossword-puzzle book. What in the world did the man do for entertainment?

He glanced at his watch for the hundredth time since leaving the mansion. Four o'clock. At this rate, he'd wear out the cabin's wooden floors before nightfall with all this pacing. Maybe Danae was still at the house. If so, he could always ask if he could take an inventory. That way, he could pick up any needed supplies in order to begin work straightaway the next morning. Surely she couldn't find fault with that logic.

Mind made up, he grabbed his keys and headed back to the mansion. As he pulled into the drive, he saw a truck with the sheriff's logo on the door. His hand tightened on the steering wheel as he pulled behind the truck and parked. What could be going on that warranted the sheriff?

He hopped out of his truck, and as he started toward the front door, it opened and a man stepped out. Zach studied the sheriff as he approached the entrance. This athletic man looked to be about the same age as him, the last thing he'd imagined for the sheriff of Calais. An aging, balding man with a potbelly was more what he would have guessed.

The sheriff caught his gaze immediately as he stepped outside and glanced back at Danae, who stood just inside the door. She said something to him and he nodded then made his way across the drive, meeting Zach halfway.

"Carter Trahan," the sheriff said and extended his hand.

"Zach Sargent," he replied and gave Carter's hand a firm shake. "I hope there wasn't any trouble here."

"Not at all. I promised Alaina I'd check up on Danae."

"Alaina?"

"Her sister." Carter grinned. "And the woman most likely to make my life miserable if I don't follow her instructions."

Zach smiled. "Is Alaina as attractive as her sister?"

"Ah, now, see, I can't answer that question without being in trouble with someone, so I'll just say they're both gorgeous in their own right and leave it at that."

"You're a wise man."

Carter nodded. "Danae tells me William hired you to make the repairs."

"Yeah," Zach said. "I just got a glance at the inside earlier, but it looks like my work's cut out for me."

"Definitely." He studied Zach for a moment. "This seems an odd choice of jobs for someone as young as you. I figured the reconstruction in New Orleans pays better and offers the nightlife."

The delivery of the statement was casual, but Zach knew a fishing expedition when he heard it. The sheriff's seemingly pleasant disposition didn't completely mask his shrewd observation skills. Zach had to be very careful, very deliberate, around this man. If he gave Carter any reason at all to suspect he wasn't exactly who he claimed to be, he'd run him out of town on a rail.

"The rates are better, that's true. But I've been in the city all my life. Sometimes a man just needs to get away from everything—slow down a bit."

Carter nodded. "I get that. Did it myself earlier this year. Resigned my detective position with the New Orleans Police Department and came back home to run herd over a town with less people than my old apartment building."

Zach struggled to keep the surprise and

worry from his expression. A young, inquisitive sheriff with big-city experience and connections was the last person he needed looking into his background. This was no small-town sheriff that could be easily fooled. "Any regrets?"

"Not a single one."

"Then maybe I'm on the right track."

Carter smiled. "Did you get settled in the caretaker's cabin?"

"Didn't bring much with me except work clothes and some tools. To tell the truth, I was feeling kinda stir-crazy, so I came to see if Danae was still here. Thought I could put together a supply list and get it filled this evening. Save me some time getting started tomorrow morning."

"Efficient. I like that. Well, guess I'll leave you to it. Maybe I'll see you in town sometime—buy you a slice of pie and coffee down at the café."

"That sounds like the best offer I've had in weeks. Nice meeting you."

"You, too," Carter said as he strolled to his truck. He gave Zach a wave as he pulled away.

Zach looked over at the entry, not surprised to see Danae still standing there, observing the entire exchange. She frowned as Carter's truck pulled away, and Zach wondered if Danae wasn't thrilled with her sister's choice of men.

He'd seemed nice enough but a person never really knew what went on behind closed doors.

Maybe she wants him for herself.

The thought came unbidden and he felt a twinge of jealousy, which irked him. He was in Calais to find answers and then get back to his real life in New Orleans. He'd pulled major strings to manage even a few weeks away. The absolute last thing he needed to do was waste any of his precious time with amorous thoughts of a woman who seemed annoyed at his presence.

"I wasn't expecting to see you back so soon," Danae said as he approached the door, her tone telling him straight off she wasn't the least bit happy to see him, either.

"I was hoping to get a quick inventory—maybe get some of the supplies this evening."

"That's what I heard. I'm going to be here another hour or so. Do you think you can cover enough ground by then?"

He shrugged. "It will be more than I have now."

Danae opened the door wider and stepped back, allowing him to enter.

"So," he said as he stepped inside, "your sister and the sheriff?"

She raised one eyebrow. "I didn't take you for a romantic, Mr. Sargent."

"Please call me Zach. And maybe I was just interested in your sister."

She gave him the faintest of smiles. "Most men that have seen her are."

"Really? Then I guess it's a real shame she's settled on a guy who carries a gun for a living."

"You don't like living dangerously?"

Surprised at the slightly teasing tone of her voice, he smiled. "Not when it comes to women."

"Smart."

She turned and waved a hand toward the vast open entry. Zach couldn't help but notice how her jeans curved over her hips, how her T-shirt clung to her full chest and tiny waist.

"What did you have in mind?" she asked.

"Huh?" Her question came at the worst possible time, because at that moment, none of the things he had in mind had anything to do with the repairs.

"Well," he drawled, hurrying to recover, "I thought I'd do a quick inventory of rooms to note the obvious items. I'm sure the list will expand as I begin work. Is there any problem in particular you'd like me to start with?"

Danae nodded. "The power is my biggest concern. I will be working through the property records for William, and the office is one of those rooms where the power is out. I can haul the files to the kitchen to work, but it would make it easier to see in there..."

Her voice trailed off and she frowned.

"Is something wrong?" he asked.

"It's stupid."

"Why don't you let me be the judge of that?"

She stared off across the entry then finally blew out a breath before turning to face him. "It's creepy, okay? I know that sounds foolish and girly and weak, but the room is creepy and the lack of lighting makes it worse." She dropped her gaze to the floor.

"It doesn't sound foolish or weak at all. For my own well-being, I'm not touching the 'girly' comment." He scanned the cavernous room, littered with columns with various sculptures and statues—all covered with layers of dust and cobwebs. "Look, I'm sure this place was beautiful once, but I have to tell you, it wouldn't be someplace I'd choose to stay."

She looked up at him, a flicker of appreciation in her expression. "Really?"

He held up one hand. "Swear. This place is gloomy and depressing. Your sister's work in the kitchen gives me an idea of what it could look like, though."

Danae gave him an appreciative smile. "You're right. I need to keep reminding myself that it will feel different after the repairs are made and we've managed a good scrubbing."

"It's none of my business, but why doesn't William hire someone to do the cleaning?"

"According to café gossip, he's tried, but none of them last more than a day."

"Why not?"

She smiled. "Because of the ghost."

Maybe it was the decrepit state of the house, or maybe it was the swamp that was slowly swallowing up the entire structure, but he actually gave her statement more than a moment's passing thought.

"Ghost, huh?" he said finally.

"That's what I hear."

"But you haven't seen it?"

"No, but then today is the first day I've been in this house since I was a toddler."

He wanted to ask her more about her stepfather and her sisters, but as soon as she'd issued that statement, her expression had gone from somewhat relaxed to completely closed off again.

"Who's the ghost supposed to be?" he asked instead.

She frowned. "I don't know. I assumed it was my stepfather. Based on the description of his lifestyle from the locals, it sounds like he was agoraphobic. I guess I figured that even in death, he didn't want to leave the house."

"Well, then, I guess I best get to work lighting up this place before I have to add a ghost to the payroll."

Danae gave him a small smile, but he could tell that something was bothering her. She appeared to be telling the truth when she said she hadn't seen a ghost, but something had happened that put her on edge—something beyond just a spooky house. She was too observant, too suspicious for the average person. Either she was paranoid or she had something to worry about. Both concerned him as either could blow his cover.

"Where would you like to start?" Danae asked.

"Well, I know the electricity is a priority, but I need to test everything before I can pin down the problem. I brought my voltage equipment with me, so I'll start that tomorrow morning. I thought I'd take a tour of the house and note the obvious needs. Then I can have supplies on hand for several jobs."

Danae nodded. "So if you have to wait on special orders, you can keep working on other things."

"Exactly."

"Then I guess we can start downstairs."

We? The last thing he needed was the cagey

heiress lingering over his shoulder while he cased the house, especially now that his mind had formed a permanent imprint of her absolutely perfect rear end. But before he could formulate a logical argument, she spun around and headed to the kitchen, then came right back with a pad of paper and a pen.

"It will probably go faster if you dictate as you go," she said. "I can make the notes. That way you don't have to stop what you're doing to write."

He nodded, unable to argue with the efficiency her plan presented. "I assume you have a basic idea of the layout, so lead the way."

She pointed to rooms that lined the south side of the house. "We can start over there and work our way around."

He followed her into the first room and was pleased to find it only contained a table, dresser and a couple of boxes. The west window was intact, but a sheet of plywood covered the wall where he guessed a south-facing window was located. "What happened here?" he asked, pointing to the plywood.

"I haven't asked about it yet, but I assume the guy who attacked my sister broke it to get inside. The plywood covering it looks new."

He stared at her. "Someone attacked your sister in the house?"

"Yeah." She frowned then shook her head. "I guess I forget it's just hitting the news this morning. He attacked her here but she ran into the swamp and got away. He caught up with her trying to get away in her SUV, and that's when Carter shot and killed him."

He stared at her for a moment, trying to absorb the implications of trying to keep his cover intact at a crime scene. This entire situation was becoming more complicated by the minute. "Wow! Is she all right?"

"She's fine." Danae cocked her head to the side and studied him for a moment. "Most people would ask who was trying to kill her and why."

"You said it just hit the news. I can catch up on the local gossip later. I have a younger cousin who's more like a brother to me. I guess I was thinking about something happening to him."

"Are you always this logical?"

"I try to be. It seems to make life easier."

"Well, then, I guess we best get back to this list. I don't want to throw you off course."

He crossed to the intact window and studied it. "I'll have to remove the plywood to check the dimensions, so I'll leave off replacing the window for later. I'm going to have to special-order something to even come close to matching the others, but I know a guy in New Orleans who specializes in making windows for restoration projects. I can get some pictures tomorrow and see what he can do."

He reached up for the latches and opened the window, then pulled it upward, but it stayed firmly in place. It only took a moment to realize the sliding pane of the window had been nailed into the frame. The oxidation on the edges of the nails let him know that wasn't a recent addition.

"This window is nailed shut," he said.

"Yeah. They all are. I suppose my stepfather was agoraphobic *and* paranoid."

"He didn't want out and didn't want anyone else in." He shook his head. "That's no way to live. I'll remove the nails tomorrow—test all the windows and make sure they lift properly."

"No!"

The single word came out with such force that he spun around, surprised. She stood with her arms crossed. Her face was slightly flushed and her jaw set in a hard line.

"I can't test the windows if they're nailed shut."

"Then I guess they won't get tested—not as long as I'm working in this house. At least this way, if someone wants to get in here, I'll hear them coming or see the results of their attempt the next morning. What I don't want is for someone to have the element of surprise."

He studied her for a moment. Had he misjudged her? He'd thought her suspicious and hypercautious, but could Danae be tipping into the same realm of madness that her stepfather had lived the last of his life in?

"Are you expecting trouble?" he asked.

"No," she said a little too quickly. "It's just that the house is full of valuable antiques and if word gets out it's empty at night..."

She was lying. She was very, very good at it, but he'd employed too many ex-cons to recognize a snow job when he was getting one. The house *was* full of antiques, and he suspected a lot of them were valuable, but that wasn't the reason she was worried about intruders.

Maybe Danae had brought trouble with her to Calais. Maybe she was afraid that trouble was about to catch up with her. Either way, in addition to tiptoeing around with his own agenda, he was going to have to constantly look over his own shoulder, watching for whatever the heiress was hiding from.

"Okay," he said finally. "It's your house."

He motioned to a door in the corner behind her. "Bathroom or closet?"

"Closet, I think. I'm sorry. There're so many rooms, I haven't gotten everything straight yet."

She turned and pulled the door open. As soon as she did, a stack of boxes tilted out and toppled onto her, sending her reeling backward. Mice scattered across the floor, scurrying in every direction, looking for an escape.

He rushed forward, catching her before she crashed to the ground. She'd twisted her body in anticipation of the fall, trying to reach for the floor before slamming into it. Now she was gathered in his arms, the front of her toned, curvy body pressed against him. That beautiful face looking up at him—so strong, yet vulnerable.

It was a bad idea, but before he could talk himself out of it, he lowered his lips to hers.

Her lips were soft and pliant as he caressed them with his own, and he felt a surge of excitement go through him that he hadn't felt before from a simple kiss. He pressed harder, deepening the kiss, and was almost surprised when she responded, her lips searching his.

Then suddenly, she jumped up and backed away from him, one hand over her mouth. She stared at him, her face flushed, her expression a mixture of shock and anxiety.

"You should finish this yourself." She whirled around and practically ran out of the room.

He stared at the empty doorway, trying to decide if he'd been a genius or a fool. On one hand, he'd probably prevented her from asking more intrusive questions about his life. Clearly, she wanted to avoid anything personal.

On the other hand, he'd enjoyed that kiss entirely too much for his own comfort.

Get in gear, Sargent!

He grabbed the paper and pen and hustled out of the room, his mind suddenly latching onto the golden opportunity she'd presented. For the first time since he'd entered the property, Danae wasn't looking over his shoulder. She was flustered enough to rush off, so with any luck, she'd remain far away until he sought her out. That gave him a window of opportunity to create an entry into the home.

The one functional window in the first room had led straight into a huge, thorny rosebush, so it wasn't an option. He hoped his luck would be better in the second room, but it had furniture and boxes stacked to the ceiling and he could barely squeeze inside. No feasible way to reach the windows existed, so he continued to the next room. This one wasn't quite as cluttered, but it still contained stacks of paper, boxes and small furniture. He lifted several boxes away from the wall where he guessed the window was located and was pleased to find only two nails through the frame.

He hurried back to the doorway and glanced around the entry, then pulled out his pocketknife and began working the first nail from the frame. Every time the knife blade slipped from under the nail's head, he mentally cursed and wished for the pry bar in his truck, but no way was he risking the opportunity by leaving the house to get it.

Finally, the first nail worked out of the frame and he checked the entry again before starting on the second nail. This one was deeper, leaving creases in the hardwood where it had been pounded into the frame, and he struggled to get even a tiny piece of his knife blade underneath.

Suddenly, there was a loud thud overhead and he froze before closing the pocketknife and shoving it into his jeans pocket. Then he dashed back to the front of the room and grabbed the paper and pen. He peered out the door, but saw no sign of Danae. Then a second thud echoed across the entry from above, letting him know someone was moving around upstairs.

Surely it was Danae working upstairs. He started to run back to the window to finish up but hesitated. Seconds later, Danae rushed into the entry from the kitchen hallway, her eyes wide.

Chapter Six

"Did you drop something?" Danae asked, her voice shaking slightly.

Zach shook his head and put one finger over his lips then pointed at the ceiling. Her eyes widened and she sucked in a breath. Then the split second of fear was gone and her expression hardened as she pulled a nine millimeter from her waistband.

He didn't even bother to control his surprise. Minutes before, he'd had the woman wrapped in his arms and hadn't even known she was packing serious firepower. Before he could even formulate a plan, she slipped silently across the entry and up the staircase. He hesitated only a second before hurrying behind her, cursing that his pistol was locked away in his truck along with his pry bar.

He caught up with her at the top of the stairs and pointed at the far end of the hallway to the right, where he thought the noise might have originated. She nodded and hurried down the hall, using the carpeted runner in the middle of the hallway to mask her footsteps.

Zach peered into each room as they passed, but if anyone was hiding inside, it would have taken more than a peek to discover them. The rooms were just as crowded with boxes and furniture as the downstairs rooms he'd seen. As they reached the last door, Danae stopped and looked back at him. He gave her a nod, and she sprang around the doorway, gun leveled.

He was only a millisecond behind her, but his expertly executed timing was useless. This time, it was clear the room was empty, even with only the dim lighting from the entry to illuminate it. Purcell's office, he thought, as he stepped inside. A huge ornate desk stood in the center of the room, a massive chair with faded, cracked leather positioned behind it. The walls were completely covered with bookcases that were overflowing with books and paper. Plastic containers, also filled with paper, littered most of the floor, leaving only a narrow pathway behind the desk and to the far corner.

"That's the entry to the master bedroom," Danae whispered and pointed to the corner where the path ended.

He squinted into the shadows and realized

that the last bookcase didn't meet quite right with the back wall. He stepped across the room and peered into an even darker room beyond the office, unable to make out anything but the faint form of bedroom furniture.

"Do you have a flashlight?" he asked.

"Downstairs, but it wouldn't matter. If anyone was here, he's gone now."

"Gone where?"

"There's a servants' staircase at the back of the bedroom. It leads downstairs into the hallway off the laundry room. I found it earlier today."

Zach clenched his pocketknife, trying to process the information. "Something caused those thumps and it wasn't footsteps."

He walked back across the office, scanning the floor as he went, then indicated two cardboard boxes dumped sideways on the floor at the edge of the desk. The sides were split in two and the papers inside were scattered across the floor.

"Maybe it was those boxes," he said.

Danae looked over at the boxes, then up at the desk and nodded. "I saw those there earlier. I intended to take them home with me tonight."

"Did you place them too close to the edge?"

She stared at the desk and frowned. "They

were already there, but maybe they were close to the edge. I was distracted when I was up here."

He nodded. "Yeah, I can see why. You were right."

"About what?"

"This room *is* creepy." He fingered a stack of papers hanging off the end of a bookcase, suspended in place by a paperweight. "It's like looking at the culmination of one man's madness. I'm guessing the bedroom is no better."

"I've only seen it by flashlight, but I'm going to go with a 'definitely not better' on that one."

Zach ran one hand through his hair and blew out a breath. "Let's go check the doors downstairs—make sure they're all still locked."

"Good idea." She grabbed a stack of the files from the floor and rushed out of the office like a shot.

Zach gave the gloomy room one more glance and hurried behind her. He hadn't been lying to pacify her. Something about those two rooms felt off. Since he'd taken his first step inside, he'd had the overwhelming feeling that he needed to leave. He was glad he didn't have to ignore it any longer.

Danae led the way, and it only took minutes to check the downstairs doors. Only minutes to ascertain that all were locked tight and showed no signs of recent passage. Danae stepped out of the laundry room and walked slowly back to the entry, frowning the entire way.

"Maybe the boxes were too close to the edge of the desk," she said finally.

"You didn't think so earlier."

She blew out a breath, clearly frustrated. "I can't be sure. I told you earlier I didn't like the room. I know it's stupid, but I accidentally moved them earlier when I was doing a cursory review. Maybe I wasn't paying attention like I thought I was."

"Maybe," he agreed, but he wasn't convinced that was the case.

"That has to be it, because there's no way he could have left the house." She nodded. "That's got to be it."

She shoved the pistol back into her waistband. "If you don't mind, I'd like to go ahead and wrap things up here. I have some things I need to take care of this evening."

"Sure."

She gave him a nod and started down the hall toward the kitchen. Zach watched her walk away and frowned. He wasn't at all convinced that she'd moved the boxes too close to the edge, but he wasn't about to tell her his theory.

That whoever was upstairs was still in the house.

DANAE PULLED UP in front of her cabin in the woods and hurried inside. As soon as she pushed the door shut behind her, she shoved the dead bolt into place and leaned back against the old wooden frame, taking a minute to catch her breath. She'd seen nothing when she pulled up in front of the cabin, nor while she dashed inside, but she couldn't seem to shake the panicked feeling she'd carried with her most of the day.

She pushed herself away from the wall and walked the few steps into the tiny kitchen to dump a stack of files from the house on her breakfast table. Only yesterday, she'd restocked her refrigerator with bottled water, and she pulled one out and took a big gulp, the cold liquid burning the back of her dry throat.

The events of the day raced through her mind on high speed. Had it really been only a day? So much had happened that it seemed as if it had taken far longer than the mere ten hours that had passed since she'd burst into William's office and announced her true identity.

You're losing it.

She didn't want to believe it—didn't want to think that the girl who had lived on her own at fifteen was falling apart over a spooky old house and an unlocked door. But as hard as she worked to dismiss everything as oversight and an overactive, overly stressed imagination, she couldn't ignore the fact that her entire mind and body screamed at her that something wasn't right.

Maybe some of the things that had happened today had been coincidence—like the boxes falling in the office. But what about the open laundry-room door she'd found earlier that day? The one that had prompted her call to Carter?

He hadn't taken her concerns lightly, nor had he even remotely appeared as if he thought she'd imagined the entire thing. In fact, he'd been adamant about not wanting her in the house alone and had appeared relieved when she mentioned the contractor who would be starting work there the next morning. Carter was logical, direct and not prone to fanciful thinking. If he wasn't willing to dismiss what she'd found, then she shouldn't be, either.

Then there was Zach Sargent. He certainly didn't look like any contractor she'd ever known. With his lazy smile, long eyelashes and chiseled features, he looked more like the privileged boys she'd served coffee and Danish pastries to at a swank eatery in Los Angeles, just a block away from one of the best private schools in the state. Certainly, he was the last thing she'd ever expected to see deep in the swamp.

And I kissed him.

She chugged back another gulp of water then poured some of the icy liquid across her clammy forehead.

What in the world was I thinking?

His kiss had been completely unexpected, but it wasn't the first time something like that had happened. Years of bartending and waitressing had left her with a history of lip-locks that she'd never have chosen for herself, and heaven knew it had gotten harder and harder to fend off advances from her drunken custodian's strung-out boyfriends, which was what prompted her to finally leave and go it alone before she was legally able to do so.

But never, in all those years of sneak attacks, had she kissed someone back.

For the first time since she was a teen, she'd lost control. And even that split second of loss had her fuming. She couldn't afford distraction, and certainly, she couldn't afford to let her guard down. Something was going on in that house. And even though she had no doubt Carter would be keeping a close watch on her, he had a job to do and couldn't stand guard over her all day.

Because he knew it as well, Carter had tried to talk her out of working at the house, volunteering to transport the paperwork to her cabin. She'd been tempted, but then that left the contractor roaming the house, unsupervised, and for some reason, she hadn't liked that idea. Now she didn't like the idea of *her* roaming the house with the contractor loose. Clearly, she'd lost all control where sexy Zach Sargent was concerned.

Alaina.

She reached for her cell phone, chiding herself for not thinking of her sister straightaway. Alaina had lived in the house for two weeks, and she was no stranger to danger or the general feeling of unease. Danae clearly remembered the morning Alaina came into the café before dawn—after the first night she'd spent in the house. Her face had been pale and drawn, and when Danae had quipped that she looked as if she'd seen a ghost, Alaina had spilled coffee on herself.

Then earlier her sister had made the cryptic ghost comment before she had to rush off the phone. Danae didn't believe in ghosts for a minute, but she did believe someone was in the house—someone that Alaina had probably misconstrued to be a ghost. It was easy to understand why. Danae didn't feel comfortable in the house during the bright light of day. She couldn't fathom spending nights there alone.

Her sister had some serious backbone.

Danae smiled, happy in the knowledge that

her sister was such a strong woman. Danae admired and respected strong women and was happy that she wouldn't have to pretend to like some shrinking violet.

But as she studied her cell phone, her smile turned to a frown. No service. She should have figured. With the storm brewing overhead, reception in the swamp would be sketchy to nonexistent. She put the phone down and tapped the counter with her short fingernails until the clicking noise irritated her enough to stop.

She could drive into town and see if her cell phone could get service there. And although Johnny wasn't thrilled that she'd quit her job at the café, he'd allow her to use his landline to call Boston and pay him the charges when the bill came.

But to what end? Did she really think Alaina had the answers? Surely not, or she would have already shared them with Carter and William.

You want to feel close to her.

The thought ripped through her mind and she clenched the counter, that reality such a stark contrast to the rest of her twenty-seven years. She'd deliberately avoided creating lasting relationships. It hadn't been hard. Most people she'd come across couldn't be trusted anyway. But now, with Alaina, Carter and William, she'd found herself struggling to keep her guard up, while her heart pushed back, wanting to trust, wanting to attach.

She'd never realized how lonely she was until now. Until she'd met people she could be herself with. People who cared about her and would protect her.

A single tear fell from her eye and slid down her cheek.

Was this really the start of a normal life, with friends and family? She was scared to even dare and hope. Those desires had been pushed so far back for so long, she hadn't even realized they were still inside her.

She stared out the tiny kitchen window into the tangle of swamp that encircled the tiny cabin and sighed. What she needed was a long soak in the tub, a glass of wine and to get her head on straight. Her past was full of more difficult situations than this.

One randy contractor, a fake ghost and an unlocked door were not going to prevent her from gaining the life she'd always craved.

Chapter Seven

Zach parked his truck in front of the café and strode inside, still frustrated over the way his evening had gone. After checking the doors, Danae had insisted they clear out of the house for the day. Unable to formulate a good argument for insisting she stay when she was clearly distressed, he'd simply agreed and watched as she locked up the house and drove away.

He'd had no opportunity to finish his work on the window, so that one nail still held it fast in place. Tomorrow, he'd bring his crowbar and make quick work of it as soon as he had the opportunity, but that left him with a long night of nothing stretching in front of him.

Before his dad's death, he'd always prided himself on his patience. The intricate carpentry work he did required tons of it, as did dealing with frustrating clients that changed their minds every other day. But ever since his dad's funeral, he'd been unable to focus on his work—

unable to stop the feeling of dread that flowed through him when he wondered what his dad had hidden from him.

Now he was in Calais, working at Ophelia's house. But, at that moment, he was just as far away from answers as he had been in New Orleans.

Sighing, he took a seat on a stool at the empty counter. Every table save one was occupied and the volume in the small building was fairly loud and cheerful. All around him, people relaxed and shared their day with spouses, friends and children, but relaxation and sharing were the last two things on his mind. The only person who looked unhappy was the cook, who glanced back with a half scowl when Zach slid onto the stool.

"Mind if I join you?"

A voice sounded behind him and he turned just as Carter sat on the stool next to him.

Before he could answer, a perky brunette stepped in front of them. "What can I get you two?"

Zach glanced at the menu printed on the wall behind the counter then looked over at Carter. "How's the chicken-fried steak?"

"Fantastic," Carter replied. "Make it two of the chicken-fried steak. And two beers. On me."

"That's not—"

"No arguing," Carter said. "It's the least I can do your first night in town. Might as well have a good meal and general conversation before you have to head to Amos's cabin and spend the rest of the night bored to tears. How anyone lives without a television and the internet is beyond me."

Zach smiled. "Well, I appreciate it—the food *and* the conversation."

"Did you get your supply list?" Carter asked.

"No. I got interrupted and we called it a day."

Carter frowned. "What kind of interruption?"

"A couple of boxes fell off the desk in Purcell's office. It shook Danae up a bit."

Carter's jaw flexed and he stiffened on the stool. "You sure they fell?"

"Far as I could tell. We checked the doors and they were all locked from the inside. No one was in the house besides Danae and me, and we were both downstairs at the time."

Carter studied him as he delivered the information, and Zach wondered why the sheriff looked so concerned over something that sounded so simple. Suddenly, he had the overwhelming feeling that both Danae and Carter were keeping something from him, and he didn't like it one bit.

"Any reason why you think they didn't fall?" Zach asked.

Carter stared at him for several seconds, and Zach could tell the other man was deliberating whether or not to tell him something. Finally, Carter nodded.

"I wasn't at the house today just to check in on Danae. She called me because she thought she'd seen someone in Purcell's office. She found the back door in the laundry room unlocked, but Danae was certain she'd checked it earlier and it was locked."

"I see." Finally, Danae's edgy behavior began to make more sense. "Why didn't you tell me earlier?"

"She asked me to keep it quiet, and besides, I didn't really know you then."

"You don't know me now."

Carter grinned. "That's true, but I could tell you were bothered by the noise and you took her seriously about checking for an intruder. That tells me you have a problem with people who might try to scare women, and since you'll be in the house all day, I figure it doesn't hurt to have you paying attention."

"You think someone is trying to scare her?"

"Maybe. I'm not sure how much you heard about the business with her sister Alaina."

"Only the little that Danae told me—that she was attacked in the house and you shot and killed her attacker."

"That's the short version, but there're a couple of things that still don't sit right with me."

"Like what?"

"One night someone broke one of the downstairs windows."

"I saw the window you're talking about when I was making my list. Danae assumed Alaina's attacker got in that way."

"He wanted us to think that, but the window was broken from the inside, and it was still nailed shut. He didn't do his homework on that one, and I didn't let that information leak out."

"Then how did he get in?"

"If I had to guess, I'd say he was already in there when we arrived. I changed the back door and patio locks that night, but he could have been hiding there already. Quite frankly, he could have remained hiding there even after I went looking for him."

"It wouldn't be hard to remain unseen in that mess," Zach agreed.

"Exactly, but the story gets worse. Everyone's assuming the guy I killed broke the window, but there's no way he could have. The night that happened, he was in Baton Rouge at a charity event with over a hundred witnesses."

Zach frowned. "And you have no idea who did it?"

Carter shook his head, but something in his

expression made Zach wonder if the sheriff had his suspicions. "So you think someone has their own purpose for lurking."

"I have to wonder. First Alaina and now Danae are swearing they saw someone in the house. I don't like to think either of them is imagining it."

"But after what happened to Alaina, wouldn't Danae be on edge? I mean, they're sisters. I assume they're close."

"Not at all. Until this morning, Alaina didn't even know Danae was her sister. None of us did. When Danae came to town, she did it under an assumed name and took a job waitressing at this café."

Zach stared at Carter, confused. "Why weren't they in contact before? Are you telling me Alaina didn't recognize her own sister?"

"That's exactly what I'm telling you. When their mother died, Purcell shipped the three girls off to distant relatives at all ends of the country. They had no way to contact each other. Alaina wrote letters to Purcell once she was older, trying to find her sisters, but he never answered. Danae was only two years old when their mother died. Alaina was only seven."

Zach felt a ball of anger form in his stomach and he clenched his jaw. His mother had passed when he was five, but at least he'd had his father. Those girls had been pawned off on strangers. "What a worthless son of a bitch."

"We are in complete agreement on that point."

The cook shoved two plates of food onto the sideboard and threw a dish towel onto the counter. "I'm going on break," he barked at the waitress as she came to deliver the food. He pushed past her and shoved open the back door, scowling at them before he slipped through the opening.

The waitress slid two plates covered with huge chicken-fried steaks, mashed potatoes and corn in front of them. "You two going to stop jawing long enough to eat?" she asked and grinned.

"Oh, yeah," Carter said and managed a smile.

"You got a problem with the cook?" Zach asked after the waitress walked away.

"You noticed that, huh?"

"I thought he gave me a dirty look when I sat down, but now I realize you were walking up behind me at the time. Since I've never met the man, I'm assuming the look was for you."

Carter nodded. "It was for me, all right, but don't think he's going to be any happier with you. Jack Granger spent twenty years playing errand boy for Purcell, who apparently promised him untold riches when he died."

"But the money wasn't Purcell's, right? I

mean, that's what I gathered from William when we spoke about the situation in regard to the condition of the house."

"It was never Purcell's to give, but that didn't stop him from making promises. Jack recently took up with a widow with a sick girl. He was counting on that money to pay for medical care they can't afford."

"That sucks." Zach's heart went out to the surly cook and the sick girl.

"It does," Carter agreed, "and I was ready to feel all kinds of sorry for him but then he started drinking again. And when Jack is drunk, he's stupid and mean."

Suddenly, Zach understood what Carter was getting at. "You think he might be behind the break-in?"

"It's crossed my mind more than once. Especially as he threatened to 'show us all' when I tried to talk some sense into him."

"You think he's trying to scare them away from their inheritance? Would he get anything?"

Carter frowned. "I don't know what happens to the money if the sisters don't meet the terms of the will. That's something that I was going to cover with William, but everything with Alaina went down before I got to it. I hoped that it was all over with her situation, but the facts show that something else is going on in the house."

"And you're sure he's capable?"

"More than. He's tolerable when he's sober, but he's never been what you'd call a nice man."

"If it's him, what's his goal?"

Carter shook his head. "Maybe to scare them away, figuring if he can't have it, no one else should. Maybe just to steal some things he thinks are valuable and try to sell them, and they're in the way of his doing that."

"The house is crammed full of stuff. It would be impossible to know if something's missing."

"Yeah, that's the reason William has Danae going through Purcell's records. He's trying to put together an inventory of potential valuables so they can attempt to locate them in the mess."

Zach mulled over the information. All of it had been delivered in a very straightforward manner, but something was missing. Suddenly, it occurred to him.

"So if the guy you killed didn't break the window and you changed the locks, how did he get into the house later to attack Alaina? I didn't see any damage to the exterior doors and they looked like the originals."

Carter's expression darkened and he leaned over a bit toward Zach. "That's the sixty-four-thousand-dollar question," he said, his voice low. "I couldn't change the front-door lock. It's some antique that requires a specially forged key. I doubt there are a lot hanging around, but there's a slight possibility he could have acquired a front-door key, but we didn't find one on him."

"So you don't think that's the most viable option?"

"Honestly, I don't know what to think. By the looks of things, Purcell was a secretive and paranoid man. I wouldn't put it past him to have a secret entrance to the house. I think he'd feel safer knowing he had an escape hatch, so to speak. But I have yet to find such an alternate entrance and haven't had much time to look."

"Was Alaina's attacker from Calais?"

"No. Baton Rouge."

"Then how…"

"I don't know. Maybe he paid someone in Calais for the information."

"And they would have just given it to him?"

"He could have drummed up some legitimate story and thrown in a wad of cash. These are simple people who barely get by. It wouldn't take much to fool many of them."

Zach nodded. "And nobody would dare come forward and admit something like that after what went down."

"Exactly." Carter sighed and stabbed the chicken-fried steak with his fork before attacking it with his knife, taking his obvious frustration out on his dinner.

Zach took a bite of the steak. It was likely the best chicken-fried steak he'd ever had, but his mind couldn't latch onto that fact long enough for him to relax and enjoy it. It was too busy spinning with all the information Carter had given him.

He'd hoped thoughts of an intruder in the house were only Danae's stressed imagination at work, but maybe that wasn't the case. Clearly, Carter was concerned, and the man struck Zach as observant and intelligent—not at all the type to be taken in by dramatics or supposition. The disgruntled cook only supported Carter's suspicions, and if Zach had to guess, he probably wasn't the only resident Purcell had made promises to.

Then there was the fact he'd revealed about Danae when delivering the rest of the story— that she'd come to Calais pretending to be someone else. For what purpose did she come here? To see Purcell, the man who'd thrown the sisters away? If so, to what end? And why hide her true identity? Danae acted like a woman who'd seen trouble in her past—could it have followed her to town, as it did her sister?

He sighed and took another bite of his

steak. Apparently, he wasn't the only one in Calais looking for answers.

DANAE STEPPED OUT of the tub and dried herself off before pulling on a thick, fuzzy robe, one of the few luxuries she'd afforded herself in the past year. She felt more relaxed, which was partially due to the hot bath, but probably mostly thanks to the two glasses of wine she'd consumed while soaking. She couldn't remember a time when she was so stressed that she'd actually gotten out of the tub for a refill, and she hoped to never experience one again.

Her mind turned to dinner as she stepped into the kitchen and opened the refrigerator to peruse her limited choices. Part of the perks of working at the café had been the free meals. Now that she was gainfully employed outside of the food industry, she was going to have to stock more than sandwich fixings and bagged salad.

She reached for the cheese and butter, figuring a grilled-cheese sandwich and chips were as good as anything else she had to choose from, and placed them on the counter next to a loaf of bread. As she reached for the skillet, which was hanging on a wall hook, her cell phone rang and she whirled around, her breath caught in her throat.

Idiot, she chastised herself as she reached for

the phone on the kitchen counter, her hour-long soaking completely undone in an instant.

"It's Alaina," her sister said when she answered the phone. "The connection is really bad here. Can you hear me?"

"Barely. A thunderstorm is moving in. You know what that means."

"Unfortunately, I do. Are you at home?"

"Yes. The contractor and I left at the same time."

"Good. I don't want you there alone."

Danae bit her lip. Should she tell Alaina about the moving shadow, unlocked door and everything else she'd encountered that afternoon? Her sister already had plenty to worry about.

"Is something wrong?" Alaina asked. "I get this feeling something is wrong."

Danae shook her head. Her sister must be absolute hell in a courtroom. "It was an eventful afternoon," she said and went on to explain everything that had happened.

"I don't like it," Alaina said when she'd finished. "Not at all. Are you sure you won't delay your two weeks until I can return?"

As tempting as that was, Danae couldn't agree with her sister's suggestion. "To what end? Then both of us would potentially be in danger instead of just one. If something is going on in the house, delaying my stay won't stop it any more than delaying your stay would have stopped things for you."

The sound of static rang in Danae's ears, and for a moment, she thought they'd been disconnected.

Finally, Alaina sighed and said, "I know you're right, and I'd be saying the same thing if the situation was reversed. At least promise me that you won't be at the house alone. If the contractor leaves to buy supplies, go with him."

Danae clutched the cell phone. The last thing she wanted to do was get into close proximity to Zach again, and riding in a vehicle with him violated the "close proximity" rule. "If I have any reason for concern, I'll leave the house when he does."

"Since we're cut from the same cloth, I'm going to assume you're as hardheaded as I am and won't bother pushing for more. But please be careful. Be watchful. It took most of my life to find you. I don't want to lose you again."

Danae's eyes moistened at her sister's words. In reality, her sister was a stranger, but apparently Alaina felt the same connection she did.

"I'll sleep with my eyes open," Danae said.

"And don't be afraid to call Carter if things feel off. He'll come without question and he won't mock you if it turns out to be nothing. He's sorta great that way."

Danae smiled, happy her sister and Carter had found each other. Danae had admired Carter Trahan, both physically and mentally, since her arrival in Calais, but she'd known right away that he wasn't the man for her. He was gorgeous and smart and all white-knighty, but seeing him didn't give her that little thrill—that spark that she knew she'd feel with the right someone.

Like with Zach.

"I will call Carter anytime I'm unnerved," Danae promised, trying to block all thoughts of Zach from her mind.

"Well, the connection is getting worse, so I guess I better let you go. Stay safe, Danae."

"You, too." Danae waited until the call dropped then placed her cell phone on the counter.

The cheese and butter still sat on the cabinet where she'd left them earlier, but all thoughts of food had flown from her mind during Alaina's call. She stuck the items back into the refrigerator and grabbed a bottle of water. On the upside, between general anxiety and skipping meals, it would be no time before she worked off those ten pounds she'd gained working at the café.

She set the water on the tiny breakfast table and slid into a chair. Her shoulder bag lay at the edge of the table, a stack of manila folders peeking out from underneath. It was all she'd grabbed from Purcell's office when she and Zach had investigated the noise. She could have made another trip before leaving, but the thought of going back into that room had overcome logic, and she'd left with only what she'd brought down that first trip.

Still, even a couple of files were enough to start working with. A couple of hours billed meant the day wouldn't be a complete loss. She pulled the folders over in front of her. A bunch of old paperwork should take her mind off things, maybe even bore her enough that she could sleep.

The first folder contained a list of household purchases made several months after her mother's death, and the costs—bread, milk, cereal, butter, toilet paper—all seemed like basic domestic stuff and not at all what William was looking for. The next five pages were more of the same, the date of the weekly trip noted in the upper left of each sheet of paper. It wasn't useful for the lawyer's purposes, but it did give Danae an insight into how her stepfather had lived.

Sighing, she flipped through the rest of the pages in the first folder, finding nothing of interest. It made no sense to her that her stepfather had access to all her mother's wealth, but had locked himself away in that monstrosity of a house and, based on this paperwork, lived on a diet of cereal and toast.

The second folder contained more itemized shopping lists, but these were completely different from the others. A quick check of the date let her know that the purchases were made months before her mother's death. The lists contained all the things she'd expect a household with three young children to have and stood in stark contrast to the lists in the previous folder.

The last pages contained in the folder appeared to be an investment account statement. Her eyes widened at the balance in the account, and she had to take a minute to remind herself that William had already told her the estate's holdings were significant. Still, hearing it and seeing it on paper were two completely different things. All her life, she'd gotten by on very little. It was next to impossible to imagine such riches that one no longer considered price.

She scanned the entries and found a few that might interest William. A vase that cost eight thousand dollars with the notation "Ming Dynasty." A two-thousand-dollar purchase for a grandfather clock. A three-thousand-dollar Persian rug.

Shaking her head, she tried to wrap her mind around the valuables the house contained under all those layers of dust and grime. Assuming the items weren't damaged, it might be akin to a museum when clean. She flipped the page over and scanned the next one, hoping to find more nuggets for William, but this page didn't contain any large expenses. She checked the dates and frowned. It was the week her mother died.

Determined not to let it affect her, she flipped to the next page and scanned until she found four twenty-thousand-dollar entries. Funeral expenses, maybe. But when she read the notations, her head started to pound. Four people's names—one of them, the woman she'd been sent to live with. No wonder the woman had taken her in.

Danae had always wondered, but now she knew. She should have known before now—everything with Rose was about money. Money or booze or a fix. But somehow, seeing it there in black and white made it all the more pathetic.

She pushed the stack of files away and took a sip of water. The apprehension she'd felt earlier had been replaced with anger. Anger at her stepfather for selling her out to a junkie. Anger at Rose for taking money for a child she never intended to care for. Anger at her mother for dying and leaving them helpless against their evil stepfather.

She rose and paced the tiny living room twice before stopping in front of the window. She pulled the thick curtains to the side and peered out into the darkness. He'd paid them off. He'd pawned off his wife's children for twenty thousand apiece.

Four entries.

The thought jolted through her mind and she frowned. Why four entries? There were only the three sisters. Danae had recognized one of the other names as the people who'd raised Alaina and assumed one of the other names was the person Joelle had been sent to live with. But why was there a fourth entry?

What else had her stepfather paid for?

Chapter Eight

Despite the heavy dinner and two beers he'd consumed at the café, Zach couldn't settle in the caretaker's cabin. In fact, he was more restless now than he'd been earlier that day. Of course, earlier, he'd thought his only obstacle was getting around Danae to search for the answers he sought. But when he put all the facts together, it looked as if he and Danae were not the only people interested in the house.

Whoever was lurking in the LeBeau mansion was brazen enough to attempt going about his business during the day, even when both he and Danae were right below. Zach had worked with enough cons to know that meant one of three things: he was cocky, he was desperate, or he was perfectly willing to kill them if they got in his way.

None were good options, especially as it further complicated his plans for sneaking into the house after normal working hours. What if he ran into the intruder when he himself was an intruder? If Danae or Carter caught him in a late-night excursion, they might look harder into his background.

He blew out a breath and stared at the old paneled wall from his resting place on an ancient, lumpy couch. Finally, he jumped up from the couch and pulled on his hiking boots. No way was he going to get a moment's rest without working off some of this energy. It probably wasn't the smartest idea, but he was going to grab his flashlight and pistol and walk down the trail to the main house.

Maybe he'd get lucky and catch the intruder red-handed—wrap things up nicely so that Danae let down her guard, giving him more room to maneuver. By the way she'd responded when he'd kissed her, he knew it was possible to distract her. But certain distractions—like the intruder—would only make the cagey heiress more observant.

He grabbed his pistol from the kitchen counter and dug his flashlight from his duffel bag, then headed out into the night.

The sounds of night creatures drifted by as he inched down the overgrown path, but the swamp wasn't as active as he'd thought it would be given the density of the undergrowth. Although he lived in the city, he was no stranger to hunting and sleeping outdoors, but this swamp had a different feel to it than any other he'd ever been in.

Logically, he should be able to attribute the unsettling atmosphere to his general unease over the entire situation, but he knew it went deeper than that. This swamp felt alive in some way. Certainly, many of the things that comprised a swamp were living plants and creatures, but it was more than that. It was almost as if the swamp had taken all those living and nonliving items and somehow created its own identity.

It pressed at him as he hurried down the path as quickly as he dared. Sometimes the dense undergrowth all but covered the path, and the last thing he wanted was to wander off the trail. The swamp was inhabited by many deadly creatures as much as it consisted of plants, water and dirt.

He felt as if he'd walked forever when his shoulder slammed into something solid. He turned his flashlight beam up from the path, thinking he'd hit a tree, but was surprised to see a stone column covered in vines. He'd walked right into the overgrown patio off the kitchen of the main house.

Although he hated to do it, he shut off the flashlight and used his hands to feel his way to the stone wall of the house. The last thing he wanted to do was alert the intruder that someone was there, watching and waiting.

He used the wall to guide him around to the front of the house then stopped at the edge of the brush just before the circular driveway. His eyes were growing more accustomed to the dark, finally able to make out the shape of the decrepit fountain. A bead of sweat rolled down his forehead and he brushed it away. The humidity was getting worse—the air growing thicker and more still, like it did before a storm.

He cursed the caretaker for not having a television, but knew that reception would likely be spotty even on the clearest night. Still, he should have checked the weather when he was in the café, which surprisingly provided free Wi-Fi. He could only guess that many homes in Calais were left stranded with no way to contact the outside world during a good storm unless they had landlines.

His back began to tighten from standing in the one position, so he squatted, letting his legs do the work for a bit. Only ten minutes passed before his legs began to tighten, so he rose back up with a sigh. Apparently twelve years of general contracting wasn't as much of a workout as his days serving as catcher on his high school baseball team.

Locks of hair clung to his forehead as the humidity cranked up another notch, and he pushed the damp strands back on his head. This was stupid. He'd let a bout of nerves and boredom override good common sense. If he started back now, he might have time to get in a shower before the storm hit and likely took out the power.

Disgusted with the situation and himself, he started to turn, but as he shifted, something moved at the edge of his viewing range. His body froze even as he yanked his head in the direction of the movement. It was impossible to tell for certain, but it looked as if something or someone was directly across from him at the edge of the driveway.

Crossing the driveway put him in the open, and although it was cloudy, the sky cleared periodically, allowing thin streams of moonlight to pass through. All it would take was a second of moonlight to give him away in the open. He took a couple steps back from the edge of the driveway and began inching around it, carefully picking each step to keep the sound as quiet as possible.

When he made it about ten feet, he stepped up to the edge of the brush again and checked for movement on the other side. At that moment, the clouds moved away and moonlight filled the courtyard, casting a dim glow into the swamp on the other side of the driveway. He strained, trying to make out any form of movement in the brush, but everything was still.

Too still.

The thought occurred to him just as a scream ripped through the night sky. He pulled his pistol from his waistband and whirled around, trying to locate the source of the noise. It was a terrifying wail—like that of a doomed soul.

Then everything went completely quiet again.

In the upstairs window of the house, a light appeared—faint at first, then growing to a pulsing mass, the size of a human. Then as suddenly as it appeared, it was gone.

He heard the footsteps behind him too late. Before he could spin around, he felt the crack of something hard on the side of his head. His temple exploded as if he'd been shot and he fell to the ground, a pair of hiking boots the last thing he saw.

THE ATTACKER HURRIED down the trail deep into the swamp where he'd stashed his vehicle hours before. He'd spent a frustrating couple of hours inside the house before he caught sight of the maintenance man lurking around outside. He'd snuck out the back door and then patiently and silently crept up behind him until he was within striking distance.

Maybe the solid blow to the head would give

the maintenance man a reason to hightail it back to New Orleans and get out of his way. He just hoped the blow hadn't been strong enough to kill him. It would be impossible to get things done with the police crawling all over the place. The last meddling heiress had brought enough trouble to town with her. It had been weeks since he'd felt comfortable returning to business.

If only Purcell would have held on a little longer, but the old bastard had managed to screw him, even in death.

THE LIGHT SHIMMERED above her and Danae reached up, trying to touch it. She didn't know why she wasn't afraid, why she didn't flee. All she knew was that the light made her feel safe and warm. It rose above her, almost to the ceiling of the cabin, and she gasped as it changed and shifted until the pale figure of a woman came into view.

Her face was familiar, but it took a moment for Danae to realize why. The woman looked like Alaina, but different.

"Mother." Danae's voice was barely a whisper.

The figure's mouth moved, as if speaking, but Danae couldn't hear even a whisper of sound.

"I can't hear you. What are you saying?"

A single tear ran down her mother's face and she began to fade.

"No!" Danae sat upright, her hands reaching for the shimmering light as it faded away.

"So close…so close…close." The whisper came as the light faded.

Danae leaped from the couch, landing on her feet with her heart beating so loudly she swore she could hear it. She blinked a couple of times, trying to get her bearings, then realized she was standing in the living room of her rented cabin, file folders scattered across the coffee table in front of her.

I must have fallen asleep on the couch. It was a dream.

But even as she thought it, she frowned. It had seemed so real—as if her mother were really there in the room with her. As if she'd tried to speak to her.

So close.

That was what her mother had said in the dream, but close to what? Close to finding her past? Close to finding herself? She'd been searching for both for so long that some days she wasn't certain exactly what she was looking for any longer. Some days, she just felt tired. Tired of being on constant alert. Tired of regarding everyone she met as suspicious. Tired of erecting walls that no one could scale.

Tired of being alone.

As that last thought occurred to her, a mental image of Zach flashed through her mind. He was one of the most attractive men she'd ever met, and in her line of work, she'd met a lot. There was something about his easy smile that made her relax around him even when her mind was telling her to keep her guard up. Something about his obvious concern that made her feel he cared.

Two stellar reasons to keep her distance from the sexy contractor.

She glanced at her watch and sighed. Not even 5:00 a.m. The café would be opening soon, but she didn't feel like having a run-in with Jack this early in the morning. Ever since Carter had filled her in on the situation with the cook and her stepfather, she'd felt bad for the man, but that didn't mean she was going to give him the chance to snipe at her. Jack hadn't been the most pleasant of people to work with when he'd thought she was just Connie the café waitress. Her emergence as Danae LeBeau, heiress, had probably tipped him right past rude and into angry.

Her pantry was sorely in need of restocking, but she could manage eggs and toast. There was no point in attempting to sleep any longer. She was too edgy—whether it was from everything that had happened since yesterday morning or the dream, she wasn't sure, but either way, sleep was a thing of the past.

She took a step toward the kitchen then froze. Was that a noise outside her cabin? It sounded like scratching. She held her breath, trying to lock in on where the noise had originated, but only the buzz of the ancient refrigerator echoed back at her. She took two cautious steps toward the living-room window and peered outside.

The morning sun hadn't yet peeked over the thick cypress trees, so it was too dark to see anything outside except for the faint silhouette of the tree line, but she felt someone there. Watching. Waiting.

She dropped the curtain back in place and crossed her arms over her chest as a chill ran through her. What did he want with her? What was he waiting for?

So close.

Unbidden, her mother's words echoed through her mind once more.

But she still had no idea what they meant.

As the sun broke over the cypress trees, Danae turned her car into the circular drive of her family home. It was barely 6:00 a.m. and she knew Zach wouldn't show up for another hour, but she couldn't sit in her cabin any longer. She was no stranger to dangerous situations, and the reality was, she was just as much a sitting duck at her cabin as she was in the house. But at least in the house, she could look for answers—try to put together the pieces of her past.

As she stepped out of her car, something out of the corner of her eye caught her attention. She looked over at the brush near the north side of the house and saw a boot sticking out of the edge of the overgrown weeds. In a single fluid movement, she pulled her pistol from her purse and took one hesitant step toward the boot.

Call Carter.

Her mind screamed at her to let the sheriff do his job, but with the cloudy sky, she knew cellphone service would be nil. If she had to drive into town, whoever was in the brush might be gone before she got back.

She began inching toward the boot. Maybe she'd get lucky and it was her intruder. Maybe he'd been struck by lightning or had a heart attack while trying to sneak into the house.

Sure, and maybe he'll have a full confession typed up in his pocket.

She clenched the pistol, silently willing her optimistic and sarcastic selves to give her a break as she stepped next to the boot and peered into the dense foliage.

Zach!

She shoved the pistol into her purse as she dropped down beside him, placing her fingers on his neck. A wave of relief washed through her when she felt his pulse, steady and strong. Some dried blood pooled on leaves under his head, and she warred with herself over whether to move him to check his head or run for help.

Then he stirred and groaned.

She placed her hand on his chest as his eyes fluttered open. "Don't move," she said.

His eyes widened and he looked wildly around but Danae noticed he didn't turn his head.

"What happened?" he asked.

"I don't know. Can you move your head?"

He turned it slowly from left to right. "It's throbbing a bit, but everything is moving okay."

"Good. Do you think you can sit up? I need to get you inside so I can take a look at the injury and see how bad it is."

He sat up okay, but when he tried to stand, he staggered a bit. Afraid he would fall, Danae wrapped her arm around his waist to steady him and guided him toward the house. At first, he was wobbly, but as they entered and walked to the kitchen, he started to steady.

He slumped in a chair at the breakfast table and she hurried to gather a wet cloth, aspirin and a glass of water. She handed him the aspirin and he swallowed them down. His hands seemed steady as he held the glass, which was a good sign.

"This may sting a bit," she said as she patted his head just above the ear, trying to remove the dried blood. "The blood is caked in your hair, so I can't see the injury. But it's all dried, so that's a good sign."

"It doesn't feel like a good sign."

"Give the aspirin time to work."

She blotted at the blood again and finally removed enough to lift his hair and get a good look at the cut. "It's a pretty good gash. About an inch long, but it's not bleeding anymore. It needs to be cleaned, though, and you might need stitches."

His eyes widened. "No. I'm sure I'll be fine if it's cleaned up."

Instantly, Danae's senses went on high alert. The man was a contractor, and based on the scars she'd seen on his arms and hands, he was no stranger to injury on the job. Was she really supposed to believe that he was scared of doctors? Something about Zach didn't add up— hadn't added up from the beginning—but she'd been unable to put her finger on what.

"How did this happen?" she asked.

His eyes flickered a little, and she knew he was trying to decide what to say. She'd altered, edited and otherwise rewrote the truth so many times before that she recognized a cover story in progress, but Zach wasn't as adept as she was. Wasn't used to lying, so he gave himself away.

"I was restless last night and couldn't sleep, so I came to the house hoping to catch the intruder in the act."

She studied his face, but all she could see was the look of failure and a bit of embarrassment. It appeared he'd decided to tell the truth, which sent her right from concerned to angry.

"You have no business poking into things you weren't hired for," she said.

"I disagree. If someone was in the house yesterday, then that means they were inside when I was working. That puts me at as big a disadvantage as you, and I don't think I should have to work that way any more than you should."

She clenched her jaw, but couldn't formulate a good argument. Zach did have the right to feel safe in his work environment, but she still couldn't approve of what he'd done, especially as he hadn't even bothered to talk to her before doing it.

"So you thought you'd do what—take a picture? It's not like you know enough people in Calais that you could identify the intruder, even if you managed to see him."

He shrugged. "I guess I figured I'd catch him and put the whole thing to bed."

She stared. "Have you lost your mind?"

He gave her a half smile and pointed to the gash. "Maybe a bit of it leaked out."

"That's not even remotely funny. You could have been killed, and don't bother trying to tell me that you fell and hit a rock. I looked and there wasn't a rock anywhere near you, much less under your head. Besides, I've seen plenty of people clocked with a beer bottle and know what a blow to the side of the head looks like."

The smile slipped from his face. "I was hiding there, at the brush in the edge of the driveway, and I saw something move on the far side in the swamp. I waited for the clouds to clear to get a better look, but he must have left by the time the moonlight came."

"And then someone hit you?"

He frowned and stared down at the floor, his brow scrunched. Finally he shook his head. "Not then. First, the scream came."

Danae's heart leaped in her chest. "What scream?"

"I don't know. It sounded like it came from inside the house, but it echoed everywhere. It was awful—like someone in agony. Then a light appeared in the top window of the house and the scream stopped. A second later, I heard footsteps behind me, but before I could turn around, he clocked me."

She struggled to process the information, trying to put it all in a rational perspective. "What kind of light—flashlight, a room light?"

"Neither. It was more of a small glow that grew in size, pulsing as it got bigger. I could see it upstairs, through the window on the landing."

"Then what was it?"

He hesitated, and she could tell he didn't want to say.

"Zach, what did you see?"

"It looked human."

Danae barely managed to keep her shock from showing. Under other circumstances, she would pass off Zach's claim as a symptom of his head injury. He'd simply seen the light after someone cracked him on the head and was confused now.

But what were the odds that they had both seen a corporeal entity on the same night? She needed to know just how bad that crack on Zach's head was.

"Are you still dizzy?" she asked.

"Yeah, a little."

"I'm going to take you to Doc Broussard."

His eyes widened. "No, I don't need to see a doctor. I'll be fine."

"I'm not asking you. You were injured on my

property while under the employment of the estate I'll inherit. It's a liability issue, so you'll see the doctor. We can wait for a decent hour to call William, but I bet he says the same thing."

Zach frowned but he'd been in construction long enough to know the drill. "Surely the doc won't be up yet, either, much less open for business."

"He's an early riser, and he's always open for emergencies. I'll call him from my car as soon as I can get a signal. Can you walk?"

He rose slowly from the chair. "Yeah, the dizziness is starting to go away."

"Good," she said.

Maybe when it cleared completely they could make more sense of it all.

Chapter Nine

Doc Broussard was a kind-looking silver-haired gentleman who smiled at Danae and nodded at Zach as they walked into his clinic. Zach's head still pounded from the hit, but he wasn't about to admit that to the doctor or Danae. If Danae even suspected he wasn't up to par, she could easily have him removed from the job, and that would ruin everything.

Doc Broussard introduced himself and directed Zach to sit on an examining table. "Looks like you took a crack to the head. William said he was hiring someone to work on the house. It wasn't supposed to work on you."

Zach glanced at Danae, but her jaw was set. Clearly, she wasn't interested in volunteering details. He didn't understand her reasons, but figured it was smart to follow her lead. Danae had lived here for six months and knew everyone. If she wanted to keep the whole thing quiet, then that was what he'd do.

Doc Broussard parted Zach's hair and studied the gash. "You've got a pretty good cut here. I could put a couple of stitches in to help it close faster. Wouldn't take more than a few minutes."

Zach looked over at Danae.

"That would be great," she said, "and please be sure to send William the bill. The estate will pick up the cost."

"Of course," Doc Broussard said as he began threading a needle. "Injured on the job and all that. Of course, this happened sometime last night and that gash was made by something smooth, like a crowbar. But I'm going to assume you have your reasons for wanting people to think he was injured while making repairs."

Danae sighed. "We've had some…unexplained things happening at the house. Zach thought he'd play hero last night and see if he could catch someone in the act."

Doc Broussard looked at Zach. "And you caught the raw end of it."

"I'm afraid so," Zach said.

"Humph." Doc Broussard shook his head and started stitching. "You're not the first to sit on my table and tell me a story about strange things in that house, and I'm guessing you won't be the last."

Danae's eyes widened. "What do you mean? Who else?"

"A couple of the women hired to clean. One had a pretty good scrape and the other bruised her knees pretty good."

"What happened to them?" Danae asked.

"They claim they saw a ghost."

Danae sucked in a breath. "I heard the rumors, but I always dismissed them as the fancies of simple minds. Was the ghost a woman?"

Doc Broussard shook his head. "They didn't specify. They said it appeared right in front of them and they took off out of the house. One fell in the entry and bruised her knees on the marble floors, and the other caught her arm on the end of one of those ornamental columns in the entry and that gave her the scratch."

Danae frowned. "William said he couldn't find anyone in Calais to clean. They were all scared."

Doc Broussard nodded. "They weren't the first to hightail it out of that house crying 'Ghost.' I guess the others managed to do so without injuring themselves. And then there was your sister."

"Alaina?" Danae stared at the doctor, her shock clear. "I never heard of anything happening to her. I mean…except for the attack."

"I think she and Carter were trying to keep it all quiet until they figured out what was going on, but she took a tumble down the stairs early on in her stay. Gave her a pretty good crack on the head, like our contractor friend here." He cut the stitching thread and patted Zach on the back.

"Were you...?" Danae's voice trailed off. "Were you my doctor...before?"

"No. Ophelia's parents had doctors in New Orleans that they'd used for years and always took her there for checkups. She did the same with you girls." He smiled. "At first, I was a bit offended, but then I noticed that a trip to the doctor always ended with a shopping spree for you girls. Ophelia always bought you the prettiest dresses."

Danae smiled. "That's a nice memory. Thank you for sharing that."

"You're welcome."

"Can I ask you another question?" Danae asked.

"Of course."

"Did you know my stepfather? I know he was private, possibly even agoraphobic, but I figure someone had to look after him when he was sick...."

Doc Broussard nodded. "I made a trip to see Trenton once a month—more if he was ill."

"Was he ill a lot?"

"Not really. If I had to guess, he was a good twenty years older than your mother and had the usual things that come with age and lack of proper diet and exercise—high blood pressure, high cholesterol and the like. Any of those combined with age and a weak heart could take someone out."

Danae frowned.

"I know you want to figure out something about your past," Doc Broussard said. "I'd want to do the same thing in your position, but I honestly don't know what I can give you."

"Surely you can tell me something about him. Anything?"

The doctor sighed. "You'd think after all that time I'd have an idea what made the man tick, maybe have an inkling of how he spent his time, but I don't. He lay there in his bed wearing striped pajamas, completely silent while I did my exam. The only time he spoke was to tell me of a symptom or ask about a dosage."

"That's just strange," Zach said.

"Definitely," Doc Broussard agreed. "He was an odd man, but I never got a handle on why."

"What do you mean?" Danae asked. "I thought he was mental."

"Perhaps. Certainly, the indicators were there, but I always wondered what would show if he'd agreed to the tests I suggested."

"You think he was faking?"

"Not necessarily. I think he was definitely

suffering under some neurosis, but there was a cunning in him—something so imperceptible in the way he looked at things that later on, you'd convince yourself you hadn't seen it."

"You think he was hiding something?" Zach asked.

Doc Broussard shrugged. "Aren't we all? But I couldn't begin to guess what secrets lay in Purcell's past that caused him to lock himself away in that house for over two decades. I'm afraid to even try."

"It sometimes seems," Danae said, her tone conveying her frustration, "that Purcell went to the grave still taking from everyone and not giving a single thing."

"I'm really sorry," Doc Broussard said and placed his hand on Danae's arm. "I wish I could give you some answers."

Danae gave his hand a squeeze. "I do, too, but I'm not giving up. I'll find them. It just might take a while."

Doc Broussard smiled. "I believe you." He walked back over to Zach and took a look at his earlier work. "Well, this guy is patched up nicely, if I do say so myself. Just keep it clean and dry for a couple of days and let me know if your headache gets worse."

"Thanks, Doc," Zach said, gently probing his head. "Hey, I'm curious. You said you didn't think I'd be the last person to sit here after being injured at the house. Any particular reason why?"

The doctor frowned. "Just a feeling, I suppose."

"What kind of feeling?" Danae asked. "Surely you don't believe those women or Alaina saw a ghost?"

Doc Broussard stared at the wall for a couple of seconds, rubbing his jaw, then finally looked back at Danae. "I guess I figure the house has been sitting there like a tomb all these years. Purcell was there, but he wasn't living so much as he was existing."

He took off his glasses and rubbed them with the hem of his shirt. "Maybe the house is coming alive after all these years…and bringing something with it."

Zach narrowed his eyes at the doctor. "You don't really believe that, do you? I mean, you're a scientist."

"That's true enough, but the swamps of Mystere Parish are different than most. Things happen in them that can't be explained in earthly ways. I figure that house has been so swallowed up by the swamp that maybe it's become like it."

Zach was momentarily taken aback. Last night, when he was walking the trail to the main house, he'd been thinking how different this swamp felt. How it felt alive. Now this seemingly sane and obviously well-educated man was saying the same thing. The problem was, it still made no sense, regardless of what feelings he might have.

"What kind of unexplained things?" he asked.

"Oh, ghostly lights and noises that can't be attributed to man or beast…the usual sort of thing you'd expect to find in an area of the country where things are steeped in lore and some still practice the old ways."

"But that's not why you think they're different," Zach said. "Is it?"

Doc Broussard smiled. "You don't miss much, do you? No, I have my own reasons for thinking the way I do. My own unexplained story."

"I'd love to hear it," Danae said. "I mean, if you don't mind telling it."

"Not at all. It was about this time twenty-five years ago and I was deer hunting. A fellow doctor friend of mine had canceled at the last minute, and my wife tried to convince me not to hunt alone, but I was determined. I was on call the following two weeks and I intended to get my one clear day in."

He stared out the window and into the row of cypress trees across the street from his office. "I was tracking a buck—a good size based on the tracks—when all of a sudden, I got the feeling I was being watched. Well, there's plenty of creatures in the swamp that you don't want keeping that close an eye on you, so I stopped short and tried to get tuned to what it was."

Zach nodded. "That's smart."

"Usually, but this time, it made me a sitting duck. There wasn't a whisper of sound, not a single insect or even a breath of breeze. It was the most silence I've ever experienced and it was unnerving because it was so unnatural. I had just made up my mind to get the heck out of there when something hit me on the back of the head and sent me tumbling down an embankment."

Danae gasped and covered her mouth with her hand.

"My deer-hunting cap probably kept my head from splitting open, but I broke my leg in three places on the way down. Put me in the hospital in New Orleans for a month and rehab another two after that so I could learn to walk again."

"You don't know who hit you?"

Doc Broussard shook his head. "That's where the unexplained part comes in. The sheriff—not Carter, as he was just a boy back then, but the sheriff then—was an expert tracker. He covered every square inch of that swamp in a mile radius from where I was hit. He didn't find a single track besides my own, and there was nothing—

not a rock or a branch or even a dead bird—to explain what hit me."

"But," Zach said, "there had to be something. You didn't send yourself tumbling down an embankment."

"No, sir, I did not. But whatever did didn't leave a trace. Now, what exists in the swamps of Louisiana that can knock a two-hundred-pound man down without leaving a single track?"

"I don't know," Zach replied.

"The answer is, nothing on this earth."

DANAE INSISTED THEY go to the café for breakfast. Zach was a little rumpled, but his clothes weren't stained, so he'd pass muster for the early-morning crowd, anyway. He needed to eat in order to take the pain medicine Doc Broussard had given him. Plus, she had an ulterior motive or two. First, she wanted to gauge Jack's reaction to her now that the gossip had spread, and second, she was hoping to catch Carter before he left for his usual rounds.

Jack glanced at them as they entered the café, then turned immediately back to the grill, but not before Danae caught his scowl. Apparently, the cook was aware of her ascension from café waitress to small-town heiress, and he looked none too happy about it.

Fortunately, Carter was sitting at the counter,

the empty plate in front of him letting her know they'd caught him just in time. She slid onto the stool on one side of him and motioned Zach to the other. Carter glanced at both of them, looking surprised.

"You two are out early," he said. His voice was casual, but Danae knew the question was in his statement.

"I was hoping to catch you," Danae said, keeping her voice low.

Sonia, the waitress who had replaced Danae, stepped up to the counter, a big smile on her face.

"Can I get you guys some breakfast?"

"Just some coffee for now," Danae said, "and breakfast in a few."

Zach nodded, cluing in to her desire to send the waitress out of earshot.

"I'm glad to see you here early, Jack," Danae said as the waitress poured them coffee.

The cook turned to glare at her then mumbled something to the waitress and stormed out the back door. The waitress slid the coffee in front of them and gave them an apologetic smile.

"Apparently, Jack went on break, so I'm glad you two don't want breakfast right away." She grabbed the pot of coffee and headed to the other side of the diner.

Danae waited until she was out of hearing

range then gave Carter a quick rundown of what happened to Zach. Within seconds, Carter's face went from early-morning blank to completely alert and concerned.

"Damn it," Carter cursed, keeping his voice low. "I have got to figure out how he's getting into the house. I didn't think many copies of that front-door key could be floating around, but maybe I was mistaken."

"There's probably not a lot," Zach said. "I know a guy in New Orleans who can make duplicates, but he has to have an original to work from. My guess is that the house only had two originals when the lock was installed."

Carter nodded. "And I figured because of the trouble and cost, servants would have received keys to the back door but not the front."

"Probably true," Danae said. "But you changed all the other door locks. Even if he has a front-door key, I seriously doubt he strolled up to the door, through the foyer and up the stairs yesterday with Zach and I right there."

Zach glanced at Carter, who frowned.

"What are you not telling me?" she asked, looking from one man to the other. "Oh, wait. How could I be so stupid? He was already in the house, wasn't he?"

"It makes the most sense," Carter said. "He might have entered the house that morning, and when you arrived, he had to wait for an opportunity to leave."

"But all the doors were locked after the boxes fell. Zach and I checked." She sucked in a breath. "He was still there. Hiding somewhere in the house while we were checking the doors. Do you think he's still in there now?"

"I don't know," Carter said. "I hope not."

He rose from his stool and tossed some money onto the counter. "I have a couple of things I need to get out of the way this morning. Eat your breakfast and I'll meet you at the house as soon as I can get away."

"Thanks," Danae said.

Carter gave them a nod and headed out of the café. Sonia stepped back behind the counter and refilled their coffee, so Danae and Zach slipped back into silence. As she was restocking the napkin holder, Jack came back in from his break.

"Do you want breakfast now?" Sonia asked.

"I'll have a vegetarian egg-white omelet," Danae said.

"Sounds good," Zach said. "I'll take the same with a side of wheat toast."

Jack shook his head.

"Is there a problem, Jack?" Danae asked, determined to get the unpleasantness out of the way.

Jack turned around and gave her a dirty look. "Yeah, there's a problem, Miss Fancy Omelet. I should have known the first time you ordered it that you thought you were too good for this town. Plain ol' eggs and bacon can't touch those heiress lips of yours or you might explode, right?"

"Look," Danae said, "I know what my stepfather did to you and it was wrong, but I had nothing to do with that. If you have a problem with the way things turned out, then I suggest you take that up with the estate attorney, but I will not take crap from you because you got a raw deal."

Jack's face flushed red. "You got a smart mouth now that you got a little money."

Anger from her entire life flooded through her, and she clenched her hands to keep from throwing something at the man she used to work next to six days a week.

"You think you got screwed? Purcell sold us for twenty thousand each. Paid strangers less than what a bass boat costs to rip us from the only home we'd ever known. If there was a way to bring that bastard back and kill him myself, I would. Damn Purcell to hell all you want, but the line starts behind me and my sisters."

Jack's jaw dropped and he blinked before

tossing his spatula on the grill and storming out of the café for the second time that morning.

It took Danae a second to realize that the entire café had gone silent. Without turning around, she knew every eye in the place was on her. Embarrassment washed over her like a tidal wave, and she grabbed her purse and ran out of the café.

Chapter Ten

Zach hesitated only long enough to toss some money onto the counter before he hurried out of the café after Danae. Her car was still parked at the end of the block in front of Doc Broussard's office, and she made it almost all the way there before Zach managed to catch up with her.

"Hey," he said, putting his hand on her shoulder. "Wait up."

"I'm sorry," she said, staring at the ground. "I didn't mean to embarrass you. I shouldn't have poked at him. He's always been mean-spirited, but I'm usually in a better place to tolerate it."

Zach felt his heart tug at her obvious distress. He put his hand under her chin and pulled her head up until she was looking at him.

"You have nothing to apologize for," he said. "Jack was out of line, and everyone in there knows it."

"I made a fool out of myself, airing my family's dirty laundry."

"You're not a fool. You're hurt and you have every reason to be. I take it you didn't know about the payoff until now?"

She sniffed, and he could tell she was trying to hold back the tears that were pooling in her eyes.

"I found a check register in the files I took home with me last night," she said. "There were four entries for twenty thousand dollars. I recognized two of the names. One was the woman who took me and the other was the people who took Alaina."

Zach stiffened. It was the same amount he'd seen in his father's records. "And the other names?"

She shook her head. "I didn't recognize them and the last is barely legible, but I figure one of them is the family that took Joelle."

Zach struggled to control his own anxiety. The last thing he wanted to do was tip off Danae to exactly how interested he was. Then another thought occurred to him. "There are only three of you, right?"

Danae's eyes widened. "Yes. Well, I guess as far as I know there are only three of us. I was too young to remember anything."

She clutched Zach's arm. "What if there was a baby? Oh, no, I need to call Alaina. Surely she would remember if our mother was pregnant after I was born."

Instantly, Zach felt guilty for causing her more distress. He put his hands on her shoulders and gave them a squeeze. "Don't outdrive your headlights. If your mother had another child, wouldn't William know?"

"I don't know. Everyone said Purcell locked us up in that house and no one saw my mother or us kids for a long time. Maybe long enough for her to have his child."

"Okay. So as soon as you think it's appropriate, you'll call Alaina and ask her."

Danae nodded. "You're right."

She took a deep breath and blew it out, then gave him a small smile. "Thank you."

"I didn't do anything."

"You calmed me down and reminded me that I'm not in this alone. I have Alaina and I need to remember that."

"And you have me."

Her eyes widened a bit, but he saw the flicker of hope in them before the wall went back up.

"None of this is your problem. I can't ask you to get involved. You've already done too much and you're injured because of it."

"You didn't ask. I'm volunteering."

She cocked her head to one side and studied

him for a couple of seconds. "Why would you volunteer for this?"

"Maybe because I find it all kinda fascinating, like an old movie-of-the-week story. Maybe because I always wanted to be Sherlock Holmes. Maybe because I like you and want to help."

She stared a second more then gave him a small smile. "You need to get out more. If you like me, then your friend card must be seriously low."

"There's always room on my card for beautiful maidens."

She raised one eyebrow. "Are you going to rescue me from the dragon?"

He smiled. "I didn't bring my chain mail with me, but I can have it delivered."

She laughed. "I bet you can. Well, I suppose we better get back to the house. I need to cook you some breakfast, since I'm responsible for your missing the special. Alaina stocked basics at the house. I can rummage up something."

She stepped back and out of his grasp and pulled her keys from her purse as she turned toward the car. He watched her for a moment, thinking how lovely she looked when she actually let her guard down. When she trusted someone else with a small piece of herself.

Part of him felt incredibly guilty about being one more in a likely long list of people who'd deceived and used her, but he couldn't afford to tell her his true agenda. What if his father had somehow been part of selling off the sisters? How could he expect her to remain impartial to him?

He stepped over to the car and slid into the passenger's seat. The only way this would work was if Danae never knew who he really was. After he got what he wanted, he needed to disappear back to New Orleans and forget he'd ever met her.

If that were even possible.

CARTER FILLED WILLIAM in on everything that Danae and Zach had told him at the café. The attorney's expression shifted from concerned to angry to fearful in a matter of minutes.

"Is Mr. Sargent all right?" William asked when Carter finished.

"Yeah. He took a good crack on the head, but Doc Broussard doesn't seem to think there's any permanent damage."

William shook his head. "It's like everything's repeating."

Carter nodded. "I thought the same thing. Even though I know someone else broke that window, I guess I was hoping the entire mess would go away when Alaina's situation was resolved. Shortsighted of me, I know."

"Not shortsighted. More like wishful thinking, and you can put me on the list right next to you. I really hoped all the attention Alaina's situation drew would prompt whoever else was lurking around the estate to rethink their plan. Apparently, he's as brazen as ever."

"Maybe even more so, and that's what concerns me the most. Before we latched onto the situation with Alaina, I was going to talk to you about potential suspects from an inheritance angle. We already know Jack is none too happy about the situation, but I thought there could be others. And I'd like to know what happens to the estate if the sisters don't meet the conditions of the will."

William nodded. "All very good questions, and a line of thinking I'd already taken to just before Alaina's situation was resolved."

The attorney pulled a pad of paper from his desk drawer. "I made some notes as I went through the terms of the will. First off, the cash and securities are to be distributed among several New Orleans charities and two churches."

"Are the directors of any of the charities or the ministers aware of the terms?"

"I don't see how they could be. Even if there was gossip to that effect here in Calais, it would be a long shot that any of it made it back to key people in those organizations."

"And the house?"

"The house and land, including mineral rights, would go to the town of Calais."

Carter frowned. "What was the point of that?"

"It was Ophelia's way of preserving the town as she knew it and wanted it to remain. If developers or oil companies came in, they might tear down the house and strip the land, and that would change what Calais was."

"She was assuming that the Calais city council felt the same way. They could just as easily choose to do that themselves, make a ton of money, vote themselves huge raises and bonuses, and retire in Fiji."

"Yes, that's absolutely true. I'm afraid Ophelia was overprotected by her own parents. She had the naïveté of a far younger person, and such a thing wouldn't have occurred to her."

"Does anyone on the council know about this?"

"It's quite possible. Of course, I've not told anyone the terms of the will except you, Alaina and Danae, but Purcell could have told someone."

"That wouldn't have been in his best interests, though," Carter pointed out. "If Purcell let others know he didn't have control of disbursing the estate, then people like Jack wouldn't have worked for him all those years for nothing.

Surely Jack wasn't the only one to be taken in by the man."

"No. Bert Thibodeaux was in my office a few days ago, yelling."

"Really?" Carter's interest perked up. Bert was a fifty-year-old long-haul trucker with a list of offenses a mile long. He'd even taken a swing at Carter the year before when he'd told him he couldn't park his semi on Main Street, where it blocked the alley.

"Yes, seems he did some delivery-service work for Purcell between here and New Orleans. Claims to have done quite a lot of it over the last ten years."

"And Purcell was supposed to leave him money?"

"That's his claim. Says Purcell promised him the money for a brand-new semi in lieu of charging him for all the deliveries."

Carter whistled. "There's no small price tag on those trucks."

"Definitely not."

"This is what I don't get. Why did Purcell promise them all money when he could have just paid them? Was it some perverse game on his part?"

"To an extent, certainly, but it went beyond that, I believe."

"What do you mean?"

"Purcell had access to the estate, but not in the form of large cash withdrawals. It was a very irregular arrangement, and the more I learn about it, the more I understand some of Purcell's more odd behaviors."

"Like what?"

"Like remaining in Calais, for starters. The way the estate was set up, Purcell could purchase whatever objects he desired as long as the value was sufficient to substantiate the cost, and the estate accountant in New Orleans would write a check for it. But other than a reasonable living allowance, he couldn't withdraw cash from the estate at all."

Carter leaned back in his chair and stared at William. "So he closed himself up in that house and bought a bunch of stuff with the estate money because that was the only way he could get his hands on it, then sent Bert running to New Orleans to get it?"

William nodded. "After gaining a full understanding of how the estate has been managed, that's what I believe."

"How is it that you didn't know all this before?"

"Remember, I wasn't Ophelia's attorney. Her parents established a relationship with the firm in New Orleans long before her birth, and Ophelia maintained that relationship with them. She was young when she passed. I tried to convince her to make an appointment with me and let me review all the documents, but she never did."

Carter sighed. "She didn't think she was going to die. She thought she had plenty of time to deal with that sort of thing."

"Yes," William said, and Carter could hear the sadness in the older man's voice.

"So the firm that manages the estate hired you to oversee it—is that how this works?"

"Exactly. I have formed a relationship with the firm over the years, and they felt it was a good answer to the problems created with the stipulations for the inheritance. My living here makes it easier on everyone."

"Ha, and easier for you to cajole the local sheriff into being hall monitor for the sisters."

"Yes, well…that was supposed to have been a bit easier than it's turned out to be—the hall-monitoring part, that is."

Carter held in a smile at the attorney's obvious chagrin. "You think? There's still an intruder on the loose, I've had to kill a man and now I have a fiancé. I hold you responsible for all of this."

William looked so stricken that Carter's smile finally broke through.

"I'm joking," Carter said. "About holding you responsible, anyway. The rest of it's kinda true."

William laughed, then sobered. "I know this isn't what you signed up for, and it's not what I had in mind, but I'm glad you're here in the middle of this, Carter. You're a good man and a good cop. I wouldn't trust those women with anyone else."

Carter rose and shook William's hand. "I'm going to get to the bottom of this."

"I'm counting on it."

DANAE PLACED A plate of eggs and toast in front of Zach along with a glass of milk and one of the pain pills Doc Broussard had given him. "Eat some of that before you take the pain pill," she said.

"Thanks," he said and gave her a smile. "What about your breakfast?"

"I'm too wound up to eat. I need to work off some of this nervous energy, then I'll have something."

"You sure? There's plenty here. I don't know if I can finish it all."

"I'm going to try to give Alaina a call."

"Okay. I'll be here if you need me."

She gave him a nod and left the kitchen, pulling her cell phone from her jeans pocket as she walked down the hall. She glanced at the display and blew out a breath of relief—it had a signal.

Seven-thirty a.m. She bit her lip. Alaina was

an hour ahead in Boston. Hopefully, she'd be up. Danae pressed her sister's number on the display and put the phone to her ear, clenching it harder with every ring that went unanswered.

Just when she figured it was going to go to voice mail, Alaina answered, sounding a bit breathless.

"Did I wake you?" Danae asked.

"No, I've been up for hours. My brother came this morning to take our mother to her doctor's appointment and to have her hair done, and I just finished up a quick morning run. I was going to call you later. Is everything okay?"

"Yes… No. I don't know." Danae filled Alaina in on the intruder the day before and the attack on Zach, leaving out the part about ghostly lights and terror-filled screams.

"Oh! Is he all right?"

"Doc Broussard says he'll have a headache for a couple of days, but he'll be fine."

"What did Carter say to do?"

"He hasn't said much yet, but he's supposed to meet us here later this morning."

"Good."

Danae bit her lip, trying to come up with a good way to ask her next question, but she couldn't think of one. Finally, she just blurted it out. "Did Mom have another baby after me?"

Alaina sucked in a breath. "Heavens, Danae, where did that come from?"

"Just answer me. Did she?"

"No. Not that I remember. I mean, my memories are sketchy, but I don't think I could have blocked out her having another baby."

Relief swept through Danae and she sank onto the steps in the foyer.

"You're kinda freaking me out. Why did you ask that?"

"I was going over some of the house records last night at my cabin," Danae said and went on to explain the four entries she'd discovered.

When she finished, the phone was silent for so long that Danae checked to make sure the connection hadn't dropped.

"They took money?" Alaina's voice was barely a whisper. "All of them?"

"Yeah. I saw the woman who took me listed and your parents' names and two others. You can't really read one of them anymore but I'm assuming one of the others is the people who took Joelle."

"But there were four? You're sure?"

"Positive. It's hard to miss four entries in a row for twenty thousand dollars, especially when everything else on the list was minor."

"Did you tell Carter?"

"No. I…I couldn't. It's so demeaning. I just couldn't say it out loud."

But you were able to say it to Zach.

Danae pushed that thought from her mind. Her attraction to the contractor was enough to make her uncomfortable all on its own and something she definitely didn't have the head space to address. Not right now.

"I understand," Alaina said. "But it might be important for him and William to know. They might be able to help."

"I know. I'll tell Carter when he comes this morning."

"He won't judge you. Not Carter."

Danae smiled at the absolute certainty in Alaina's voice. Her sister was already deeply in love with the gorgeous sheriff. It made Danae happy to see the two of them together—talking about building a life together. Alaina was right. Carter was a good man.

Before she could change her mind, Danae launched into her next topic. "I…I saw something last night. When you called that first time yesterday, you asked if I believed in ghosts, but then you had to hurry off the phone. I'd forgotten about it when we talked last night, but I have to know why you asked."

"Why is it so important now?"

Danae took a breath. "Because I saw something in my cabin. No one else knows, so I'd prefer if we keep this between us for the time being. I'm trying to get my footing in Calais. I don't want everyone to think I'm crazy, like our stepfather."

"Of course. Trust me, I don't want anyone to know, either. It's not exactly the thing that improves a reputation. What did you see?"

Danae told her about falling asleep on the couch and waking up to the vision above her. "I think it was Mom. She looked like the picture I have, which looks a lot like you."

"What was she wearing?"

"A long white nightgown. Her black hair hung loose around her shoulders and she was speaking, but I couldn't hear her."

Alaina sucked in a breath. "She spoke?"

"She was trying, but no sound came out until she started to fade away. Then it's almost like in my mind I heard her saying 'So close' over and over. Is that what you saw?"

"I'm sure one of the things I saw was Mom, but she never spoke. So close to what?"

"It could be anything—home, each other... I just don't know."

"I wonder..."

Danae frowned, finally focusing on her sister's very deliberate wording. "You said Mom was one of the things you saw. Does that mean you saw something else? Some other ghost?"

"Yes. That first night I stayed in the house. Remember I came in the café before dawn the next morning?"

"I remember. You'd slept in your SUV that night because something had spooked you, but you never said what it was."

"I don't know. A ghost, I guess, but it didn't look anything like Mom. This one was gray with red eyes, and there was so much anger in it. I could almost feel it spilling out on me. It looked… I know it sounds crazy, but it looked like it wanted to kill me."

Danae gasped. "Oh, no! No wonder you were terrified, and I made a joke about seeing ghosts when you walked into the café. I'm so sorry."

"You have nothing to apologize for. How could you have known? This isn't exactly the kind of conversation you have with just anyone."

"That's true. There's something else—something I left out of Zach's story." She told Alaina about the scream Zach heard right before the attack and the pulsing light that appeared on the landing.

"That scream would have sent me off on a dead run," Alaina said. "He's got some serious backbone if he stood there trying to figure that out."

Danae smiled, unable to stop from admiring the contractor's fearless if dangerous approach to problem solving. "He seems to be made of stern stuff."

"Good. Because I don't want you there alone. Not ever. Not even for a minute. And get out of that house before dark. Promise me."

"I promise. Alaina, what's happening here? What's happening to us?"

"I don't know, little sister, but we're going to figure it out."

Chapter Eleven

Carter pulled up in front of Bert Thibodeaux's run-down shack, pleased that the trucker's old rig and pickup truck were both parked next to it. It was early, but Carter wanted to make sure he caught Bert before he went out on a run. The trucker was often gone for days at a time, so it was a stroke of good luck that Carter found him at home.

He knocked on the door and waited. Nothing stirred inside, so he knocked again, this time louder. Something crashed to the floor and he heard cursing. A couple of seconds later, the door flew open and Bert glared out at him.

He was a beefy man and had a good three inches on Carter. He wore soiled jeans and a white T-shirt, but his bare feet, uncombed hair and red, watery eyes let Carter know he'd woken up Bert. The angry expression on the trucker's face told Carter exactly how Bert felt about it.

"Good morning, Bert. Can I come in? I need to talk to you."

"Hell, no, you can't come in. It's hardly a time of the morning to be entertaining. What do you want with me? Ain't no warrants out for me. All my tickets are paid."

Carter glanced behind the man into his cabin. It was a mess of dirty clothes and torn furniture. Empty beer cans, chip bags and frozen-pizza boxes littered every surface and most of the floor. A lacy red bra hung from one of the lamps, and Carter wondered briefly what kind of woman would get undressed in there. Perhaps one who'd had a tetanus shot.

Bert noticed Carter's gaze and pulled the door close to his side so that his massive body was blocking any view inside. "What do you want?"

"William Duhon tells me you used to do some work for Purcell—that you made a little scene in his office over the way the estate is being handled."

"That worthless SOB promised me the money for a brand-new rig. I ran up and down the highway to New Orleans for him for over ten years. I got a right to make a scene."

"No, you don't. William isn't responsible for what Purcell did, and he's just doing his job administering the estate. He's bound to the terms of the will, same as everyone else."

"That still don't make it right."

"I agree. None of it is right or fair, but what Purcell did to those girls after their mother died wasn't fair, either."

"I guess not, but they'll get theirs in the end. What do I get? What does Jack Granger get? All that work—all those years—and what do we have to show for it but a whole lot of nothing?"

"Would you mind telling me exactly what you did for Purcell all those years?"

Bert narrowed his eyes at Carter. "Why you asking?"

"Because some questions have arisen about Purcell's use of estate funds. I'm trying to get answers for William."

"I ain't saying nothing, then. If Purcell was up to illegal stuff, I'm not going to take the rap for that in addition to getting screwed out of a decade of pay."

"If Purcell did anything illegal, that's not on you. I'm just trying to get a better feel for the man—figure out what it was that made him tick."

Bert studied Carter for a minute, then finally shrugged. "Beats the hell out of me. He was a strange one. He bought stuff all the time—at auctions and those fancy stores in New Orleans with ugly art that costs a fortune. God only knows how much he spent on that stuff."

"So you transported the things he bought from New Orleans to here."

Bert nodded. "And back again when he sold them."

All of a sudden, Carter got it—the remarkably simple answer to the question he'd had about Purcell and the money.

"He sold the stuff he bought?" Carter asked. "You're sure?"

"I didn't see the actual things I was carrying, if that's what you mean. They were always wrapped or in crates, but nothing went inside that house that me, Jack or Amos didn't carry in, and I was the only one who made regular trips to New Orleans. He was either selling the stuff he bought or stuff that was already there."

Carter nodded. "I appreciate your time."

"Don't thank me, and tell that attorney not to thank me, either. I'm going to see a lawyer about this. I'll tie that estate up in court until those girls are dead before I let Purcell get away with screwing me from the grave."

He slammed the door and Carter got back into his truck and drove away. One question had been answered—he now knew how Purcell made money off an estate that he couldn't withdraw large blocks of cash from. But that only led to another question. Where was that cash now?

DANAE FLIPPED THROUGH stack after stack of paper, trying to find more documents from around the time of her mother's death. The lantern was the only source of light in the dark office, and it wasn't nearly strong enough to illuminate the mess that Purcell had created. She'd thought the room was cluttered, but the reality was it was practically littered with paper.

Stacks of paper covered almost every inch of the floor and oozed out of every drawer in the desk. The top of the desk was piled two feet high with folders and paper, except for the small section she'd cleared the day before to stack the boxes on. The bookcases contained few books. Mostly, they held stacks of paper and folders. Even the areas that held books had paper stacked on top of books.

It would take her forever to make sense of it all. She'd originally thought the rate for the work overly generous, but now she understood why William had to pay such an amount to get quality work. It would take everything she had not to run screaming from the mess inside of an hour.

She slumped into the office chair and assessed the small stack of papers that she'd located from the time period surrounding her mother's death. All around her were discarded piles that hadn't fallen into that time line. No one would ever guess that she'd already spent the better part of an hour digging through the mess.

"You doing all right in here?" Zach's voice sounded from the doorway.

"I guess. It's such a mess I feel like I'm spinning my wheels."

"Maybe you should try to separate it by date first, then concentrate on one piece at a time."

She sighed. "There's decades of paperwork in here. Apparently, my stepfather, my mother, my grandparents and heaven only knows who else thought they should keep every scrap of paper their hands ever touched."

Zach scanned the room. "It does look a bit overwhelming. Tell you what—I found a stack of cardboard boxes and packing tape in one of the downstairs rooms. I could line them down the hallway, and you can label them by decade or whatever works."

"That's not a bad idea. At least I'd be getting the paperwork out of the room. As it is, it's so cluttered that I can't move it far enough away to get to it all."

Zach nodded. "I'll go get the boxes."

As Zach assembled boxes, Danae lined them down the hallway, against the wall, and labeled each with a different decade spanning seventy years.

"It's a good thing we don't have to meet a

fire code," Zach said as he finished with the last box.

Danae glanced at the line of boxes that stretched almost the length of the hallway, only skipping over entrances to rooms. "I'll probably need multiple boxes for some periods, too. In fact, I'm sure of it. I don't think everything in the office will fit in the amount of boxes we have here."

Zach nodded. "I hope you wanted long-term employment when you agreed to this."

"I'm going to hazard a guess that William will say to look at the more recent time frames and forgo things that happened when my grandparents were in charge. Too many things could have happened to assets purchased that long ago."

"That's true enough. Do you want me to take a look at the electricity while you're working up here?"

"I don't want you overexerting yourself. Take it easy, at least for a day."

"The voltage meter fits in the palm of my hand and I only need to remove a couple of screws."

"Then I guess that's okay."

He smiled. "I'll go get my equipment."

Danae walked back into the dim office and sighed at the long day that stretched in front of her. She was twitchy, jumping at every little noise, and had checked her watch every two minutes since hanging up on the call with Alaina. It was almost eleven o'clock and she wondered why Carter hadn't made it to the house yet. She vacillated between hoping he'd found out something important and hoping he hadn't run into trouble.

She picked up a stack of paper on the desk and started flipping through it, checking the dates to ensure they all fell in the same decade. When she finished that stack, she placed it facedown in one of the few bare spots on the desk and picked up another stack.

The second stack of paper was also from the 1950s and she flipped it over on top of the first stack and decided to try another location. The bookcase behind the desk was crammed with nothing but paper. Maybe she would find more updated documentation there. She stepped behind the desk and slid a tall stack of papers off a shelf and carried it back to the desk.

When she saw the dates on the first paper, her pulse quickened. It was from the year her mother died, just a couple of months before. She was definitely getting closer. She flipped through the pages, noting date after date that led up until the time of her mother's death and right after. When she got to the last page, she went back to the first and started studying the transactions, but the dim light in the room made it hard to read the faded cursive.

Carrying a couple of the sheets, she walked into the hall, where the light was better. The cursive was much easier to make out, but the faded spots were many and it was still difficult for her to make out all the words. As soon as she got a chance, she'd pick up a magnifier at the general store. The store probably didn't have anything that would please Sherlock Holmes, but she knew they kept small magnifiers in stock for sewing.

From what she could make out, large deposits were made into the account randomly, and never for the same amount. Royalties, maybe? But then, she wasn't aware that Purcell had any money or investments of his own, and wouldn't royalty payments have recurring dates? She sighed and dropped the papers in the appropriate boxes, mentally adding one more thing to the list of things she needed to discuss with William. Sitting in his office yesterday, everything had seemed so simple.

Too simple.

The thought echoed through her mind, forcing her to acknowledge one of the driving mottoes she'd always lived by—if something appeared too simple, it was always going to be a bear. Still, it seemed horribly unfair that she'd come to Calais for answers and all she'd found were more questions.

"Hey." Zach's voice broke into her thoughts. "Sorry, I didn't mean to startle you."

"You didn't. Just interrupted a bunch of negative thinking that needed to stop."

He held up the voltage meter. "Well, positive or negative, I can pick up the energy signal. I'm not going to get in your way, am I?"

"Not at all, but we need to clear you a path to the light switch, unless you want to try to hook up that thing leaned over ten thousand sheets of paper."

"It's usually better to have a clear view and both feet planted on the floor when playing with electricity."

She smiled. "If we move those three piles nearest the wall, that will probably be enough. Let me grab one of the extra boxes."

She snagged one of the empty boxes from the hall and grabbed a stack of the paper and dropped it inside.

"Do you want to try to keep this in order?" he asked.

"I don't see the point. Most of the stuff I've

looked at isn't sequential. It's like God came into the office and shuffled all the paper like a deck of playing cards."

He laughed. "Now, there's an interesting visual."

When they removed the last of the large stacks away from the light switch, she dragged the box back into the hall to get it out of the way, then returned to the papers on the desk as Zach removed the plate from the light switch.

It was comforting having him right there next to her, even though she'd never admit it out loud and was a little perturbed that she felt that way. In every crisis she'd come across before now, she'd always been the strong one—the person everyone else looked to. Her own personal crisis had been borne silently and without aid, not even so much as a cry on an understanding shoulder.

It almost seemed as if revealing her true self had weakened the wall surrounding her, and now everyone and everything was systematically chipping away at it, exposing more of herself than she felt comfortable showing. For the first time since she was a child living in Rose's house, she didn't feel in control, and that bothered her.

"What the—" Zach's voice broke into her thoughts.

He was staring down at his voltage meter, a stunned look on his face.

"What's wrong?"

"It's spiking like crazy, registering way more voltage than is normally found in home wiring."

He held up the box and she saw the needle jerking back and forth in the center of the display.

"Maybe that's what is causing the problem—the wiring's shot," she said.

He raised his head and looked directly at her, his eyes wide. "You don't understand. I haven't hooked it up to the light switch yet." He lifted the loose wires up in his free hand.

She gasped as one hand involuntarily covered her mouth. It wasn't possible that the device could register electrical charge when it wasn't even connected to an outlet, but it was happening right in front of her.

"How...how can that be?" she asked, her voice barely a whisper.

He shook his head. "I have no idea. Nothing like this has ever happened before."

He moved the box around, but the needle still swung back and forth over the center of the screen. When he waved it in the direction of the bedroom doorway, it spiked even higher. He frowned and stepped toward the bedroom. When he stopped in the doorway, he lifted the two loose wires in the air and pointed them inside. The needle sprang to the right side of the meter and stayed pinned against the side, not moving at all.

"It's in there," she said. "Whatever is causing it is in the bedroom."

She looked down at the box, and suddenly, the needle fell from the right to the left. Zach shook the box and lifted the wires farther into the room, but the needle remained at zero. He stepped back into the office and walked over to the light switch, but the needle didn't move even a millimeter.

"It's gone. How can that be?" she asked.

"Given that it should never have happened to begin with, I couldn't even begin to guess why it stopped. Electricity is a moving current, but it doesn't move in those extremes—not inside of houses. And it certainly doesn't move through air."

"Except lightning."

"I didn't see any lightning in the bedroom, did you?"

"You know I didn't." She blew out a breath. "I don't know how much more of this I can take. I live a simple life, and ever since I claimed my birthright, everything has become so complicated and confusing. I'm beginning to think I should never have told William who I was and continued living a perfectly decent life as a waitress."

He placed the voltmeter on the desk and laid his hand on her arm. "We're going to figure this out."

A spark ignited in her at his touch and her arm tingled where his hand lay. It had been a long time since she'd allowed a man to touch her in an intimate way, even one as simple as a sign of reassurance, and he was the first man she actually believed when he said he'd be there for her. He was a good and honorable man who would probably do the same for anyone else, but she knew his touch held the promise of so much more.

Realizing she hadn't responded, she said, "Figuring out my problems is hardly in your job description."

He looked down at her, his green eyes staring directly into hers. "It's more interesting than repairs."

She tapped the side of her head, reminding him of his injury. "But not nearly as safe."

He stepped closer to her, and her breath caught in her throat. "Sometimes a guy just doesn't want to play it safe," he said.

She knew he was going to kiss her, and she could have moved away, but instead, her body betrayed her and leaned into him as he lowered his lips to hers. The gentle brush of his lips sent so many emotions racing through her—care, passion and desire—and she closed her eyes, drowning in this one perfect moment.

He stroked her hair and deepened the kiss, and she leaned farther into him, pressing her body against his as he gathered her in his arms. She wrapped her arms around him, her hands caressing his strong, muscular back. Her skin tingled as the blood rushed to her head, leaving her almost dizzy with desire.

"Hellooooo!" Carter's voice sounded from downstairs like a boom of thunder.

She released Zach immediately, the shock of her more-than-compliant reaction just now setting in. He held her a second longer, clearly reluctant to let the moment go, but not about to press the issue with Carter downstairs.

"Up here," she yelled as she walked out of the office and looked over the balcony. "We'll be right down."

Carter nodded. "I'll meet you in the kitchen."

She glanced back at Zach, who was staring at her with a pensive look. Was he already regretting his action?

"Should we tell him about what happened here?" he asked.

Unbidden, a flush rose up her neck at the thought of explaining to Carter what he'd interrupted, then she realized Zach meant what happened with the voltage meter, and a second wave of embarrassment washed over her as she realized her mind and body were still more engaged with the kiss and not the business at hand.

"I guess so," she said. "He won't think we're crazy. He'll just go looking for an answer. That's the way he is."

Zach nodded. "Then I guess we better get downstairs."

She hurried down the balcony hallway to the stairwell, wondering all the way just how far she would have taken things with Zach if Carter hadn't interrupted. Something told her that if the sheriff had been ten minutes later, he might have caught them in various stages of undress.

The worst part was, she was almost disappointed that he hadn't.

Chapter Twelve

Alaina LeBeau stood at the front door and lifted a hand as her stepbrother drove away. As his taillights faded into the distance, she pushed the door shut and locked it behind her, her earlier conversation with Danae weighing heavily on her mind.

She turned around and cast her gaze over the cozy living room of her adoptive parents' tiny Boston home. Real estate was at a premium where they lived and always had been. Five people shoved into twelve hundred square feet had been a challenge at times, but they'd managed to make it work, and Alaina and her brother and sister had attended great schools with stellar reputations—allowing them all to enter top-tier universities with scholarships to pay for their degrees.

Alaina had been fed, clothed, required to make good grades, praised when she'd done well and disciplined when she'd gotten out of line. On paper, she had nothing to complain about, even though she'd always known her adoptive parents never loved her as they did their own children. They cared, but that wasn't the same thing.

With Danae, Alaina got the impression that her sister's childhood had been rough, possibly even abusive. Danae had that tough outer shell and guarded her speech like so many street kids Alaina had interviewed in the past for testimony. But Alaina also knew that behind that wall her sister had erected was a vulnerable, damaged human being, and her heart ached for the sister she'd always loved and wanted to protect. Now more than anything, she wished she was back in Calais, but she couldn't see any way out of her obligations here—at least, not for a week or so.

She heard her mother shifting in her bed, trying to get comfortable, even though it was practically impossible with her broken leg. Alaina stepped into the kitchen and poured her a glass of milk and gathered her medicine. She'd made vegetable soup while they were gone and her brother had stayed long enough to enjoy the meal with them and help her get their mother settled in her bedroom.

You should wait.

The words came to her every time she thought

about the conversation she needed to have with her mother—the one where she asked if the only reason they took her in was for money. The one where she asked if Purcell continued to pay them to keep her.

She and Danae needed answers. She knew next to nothing about Danae's past, but her little sister had offered up that the woman who'd taken her was now dead. No answers were forthcoming from that source. William had yet to locate Joelle, although he thought he was getting closer. But even when their middle sister was found, no guarantees existed that her adoptive family was still alive or would be willing to answer the questions they had.

She sighed. Truth be told, no guarantees existed that her own adoptive mother would be forthcoming, but at least Alaina had the advantage of being able to read people well. She'd know if she was getting the truth or a lie. She'd know if her mother was telling her everything or holding something back, and if she had to, Alaina would twist and manipulate her into letting it all out just as she did those on the jury stand. Now was not the time to worry about past hurts. Lives were at stake.

Her mother was propped up on her back wedge, a rerun of one of those singing reality shows running on the television. Alaina handed her the milk and pills, and her mother took them both and dutifully swallowed the medicine as Alaina pulled a chair over next to the bed to sit.

"Your soup was excellent," her mother said. "I have to admit, I was a bit surprised. I don't remember you being all that interested in cooking."

Alaina smiled. "Carter's mother gave me some of her recipes and some tips. She's a genius in the kitchen and makes it look so easy."

Her mother raised one eyebrow. "So all it took was a good-looking man to get an apron on you?"

"How do you know he's good-looking?"

Her mother laughed and patted her hand. "You're a beautiful, intelligent woman, Alaina. If a man caught your attention to the point that you've got his mother giving you cooking tips, then I have no doubt he is every bit a Hollywood hero."

"You watch too much television," Alaina said, but her mother's words pleased her.

"Well, I would go bungee jumping instead, but my doctor might object."

Alaina laughed, then before she could change her mind she said, "Mom, I need to ask you something, and it might make you uncomfortable, but it's very important that you answer me honestly."

Her mother frowned. "I've never lied to you before. If I have answers you need, you'll get them."

"Did my stepfather…did he…pay you to take me?"

Her mother's eyes widened and she sucked in a breath. "Why would you ask something like that?"

"Because my sister is going through the household records for the estate attorneys and she found entries in a checkbook—large payments to you and to the woman who took her in, made just after our mother died."

Her mother sighed then gave her a single nod. "This is one conversation I hoped I'd never have to have, but I promised you I wouldn't lie and I won't. Right after your mother died, Purcell started contacting her relatives. None of us really knew your mother—her family had moved to Louisiana so long ago and never visited—but your stepfather figured family could get legal custody more easily."

Alaina swallowed. "And family who got paid for it might be willing to take on a stranger's children."

"When Purcell called us, the first thing we thought was what a horrible man, and I'll go to the grave without changing my mind on that one, but our motives weren't pure, either. We were living in a two-bedroom house on the south side of town at the time, and despite working extra jobs, we couldn't afford to get out. The school system was horrible and we worried constantly what would happen to your brother and sister if they grew up in that neighborhood."

"So you took the money."

Her mother nodded. "This house had just gone on the market, and we could stretch to make the monthly note, but we needed the down payment and money to move. Purcell's offer seemed prophetic. We needed the cash to make a better life for our own children, and you girls needed a home, but we knew we couldn't take in all three of you."

"So you got me. How was that decided?"

"We requested you because you were closest to our own children's ages. We thought it would be an easier transition for you, and we didn't want to go through toddler stages again."

Alaina took a deep breath and blew it out, trying to process the fact that she'd drawn the good family completely by default. If she'd been the youngest, she would have gotten Danae's life instead of this one. The unfairness of it all left a bitter taste in her mouth.

"Did he keep paying you? I mean, after that first payment?"

"No. It was a onetime offer and we were instructed never to contact him again. We asked for information on your sisters, but he said it was not our concern and wouldn't tell us where they'd gone."

Her mother squeezed her hand. "I'm so sorry, Alaina. It's true we made the decision to take you in because we needed the money, but I promise you we love you and are proud of you. We've never once regretted our decision."

Alaina nodded, afraid her voice would break if she spoke. She knew what her mother said was true—they did love her—but it wasn't the same for her as it was for her stepbrother and stepsister. It never could be. She knew part of that was because she wasn't their biological child, but the other part was all on her.

She still remembered her mother, and snatches of her childhood were returning to her since she'd moved to Calais. Some of the distance was her fault, because she knew where she really belonged, and it wasn't in Boston. Ever since she'd set foot in Calais, Alaina had known she was where she was meant to be.

"Are you all right?" The worry in her mom's voice was clear.

Alaina nodded and squeezed her hand. "I

don't blame you for your choices. You did what was right for your family, and I benefited from your dedication to raising your children in a safe place with a good school system."

"But you're worried about something. I've known since you walked in my door that something was wrong. I hoped with that man dead, all the trouble was behind you now."

"Apparently not." Alaina gave her mother a brief rundown of the odd things happening at the estate, leaving out anything to do with the supernatural. Her mother was a staunch believer in only what she could see and quantify.

"I don't like it," her mother said when she was finished. "Can't you girls go somewhere else until the police have figured all this out?"

"I'm not positive it would do any good. If someone simply wants to prevent us from inheriting, then I don't see any reason why the harassment would stop if we left Calais."

"But you're not safe there."

"Actually, in many ways we're safer in Calais. It's a small place, so things that are out of the ordinary are easier to spot, and Carter knows everyone and everything that goes on. He's watching everything like a hawk. He'll figure this out."

Alaina made sure her voice sounded convincing, but the look on her mother's face told her she wasn't certain.

The worst part was, Alaina wasn't certain, either.

It took the better part of an hour for Zach, Danae and Carter to exchange information, and with every passing tidbit that Carter added, Zach found himself more confused by what might be going on in the house. When Danae told Carter what happened with the voltage meter, he listened intently, occasionally asking questions, but not once did the sheriff appear even remotely concerned about their sanity.

When Danae finished, Carter looked over at Zach. "You got any idea what could have caused something like that?"

"None whatsoever," Zach said. "Unless there's a problem with my equipment, which would surprise me, I don't have a clue."

Carter nodded. "I have a voltage meter at home. I'll bring it by tomorrow for a test. I don't suppose someone could have created enough electricity in the room to set it off, could they?"

"Maybe, but our hair would have been standing on end if that much electricity was wafting through open space. And besides, the people you've got your eye on don't sound like the kind that could rig such an event, and even if they were, how would they know I'd use the voltage meter in that particular room and at what time?"

Danae's eyes widened. "You don't think he's still in the house, do you? I mean, if it was a prank of some sort, he'd have to time it correctly, but surely..."

Carter glanced at Zach and he knew the sheriff didn't want to tell Danae what he thought, but he wouldn't lie to her, either.

"Anything's possible," Carter said finally. "I wish I could tell you we're alone in the house, but the reality is, there're a million places to hide in here and no way for us to check them all. And that's just the areas we're aware of. There could be more servants' passages or secret rooms."

"Wouldn't Amos know?" Danae asked.

"No," Carter said. "I talked to him after leaving Bert's place. He knew about the servants' stairs but he has no knowledge of any exterior entries to the house other than the obvious ones."

"I hate this!" Danae jumped up from the dining chair and paced the kitchen. "It almost feels like we're being...I don't know, herded?"

Zach nodded. "Like a puppeteer—someone behind the scenes, pulling the strings."

"Exactly," Danae agreed. "Like's it all been staged just for me."

"I think it probably has been," Carter said. "Not you, personally, but the sisters."

"Do you really think a long-haul trucker or an alcoholic short-order cook could pull off something this elaborate?" Danae asked.

Carter shook his head. "But either of them could have hired someone. Or one of the organizations that will inherit could have found out about the terms of the will. It could be anyone from an employee to the board of directors to a local politician."

"Too many people," Zach said. "Too many possibilities."

"Yes," Carter agreed. "My next objective is to work on whittling down that list."

"Can we help?" Danae asked.

"Maybe. I know there are lots of options but I can't help feeling that the key to everything is Trenton Purcell. I've been looking into the man, and it's all very sketchy. It's like one day he materialized in Calais but there's not even a hint of his existence prior to then."

"So what are you thinking?" Zach asked.

"I don't have a supposition yet, but I'm hoping this house contains the answers to Purcell's secrets. Those journal entries that Danae found are a good start. Based on what I learned from William and Bert, I'd guess that what you found was Purcell's logs for his own funds."

"His accounting for the cash he made selling off estate assets?" Danae asked.

"Exactly, an entirely different issue than the estate accounts, which are managed by the law firm in New Orleans."

"Makes you wonder what happened to the cash after he died."

"Maybe that's what the intruder is looking for," Carter said. "From the looks of the office, Purcell didn't throw much away. Surely there's enough information in here to piece together what he was up to and everyone in Calais who was involved."

"Should I…" Danae began. "I guess I should start going through things in his bedroom."

A mere glance let Zach know that the last thing Danae wanted to do was spend time in Purcell's bedroom. From the weird, creepy perspective, he didn't blame her, but he couldn't afford for the voltage-meter incident to deter him from the job at hand.

"I'll do it," Zach said. "I'll search for records in the bedroom and haul them out as I find them. That way Danae doesn't have to go in there."

Danae's face flushed. "I am perfectly capable of doing the job I've been hired to do—"

"I know," Zach interrupted. "I'm not suggesting anything different, but the office is going to take forever, and I need to figure out the problem with the electricity in the bedroom anyway. Without moving some of that stuff out of there, I'll never be able to get to the sockets to test."

"He's right," Carter said. "And I'd feel better about you being in the house if Zach was nearby. The sooner we figure out what's going on here, the sooner I can make it stop. I'll talk to William and explain that Zach will be working on some nonconstruction-related things. You know he'll support that decision."

Danae sighed. "I know. We'll start this afternoon."

"Good," Carter said. "If you two are okay here, I'm going to head to New Orleans this afternoon to talk to a couple of people—see if I can turn up anything on Purcell there."

"We'll be fine," Zach assured him.

Carter rose from his chair and placed his hand on Danae's shoulder, giving it a squeeze. "We're going to get through this. I promise you."

He looked over at Zach. "Would you mind getting me a couple of items from Purcell's bedroom? Things he would have touched on a regular basis."

Zach stood, understanding immediately what Carter wanted. "You think the print will turn up something?"

"It's worth a shot."

Danae jumped up from her chair and opened the pantry. "I have some sandwich bags in here. Be careful not to touch anything yourself." She handed the box of sandwich bags to Zach.

Zach grabbed the box and headed upstairs, Carter and Danae trailing behind. Maybe this was the answer to some of the questions. If Carter could figure out where Purcell came from and why, then they might be able to get a better handle on the horrible things he did.

What worried him more was how Danae would take it if it resulted in just another dead end.

"THIS IS THE LAST of the records from the dresser," Zach said as he stacked the spiral notebooks on the desk in front of Danae. It had been a long, dusty afternoon and he wanted nothing more at the moment than a hot shower. Unfortunately, the shower was going to have to wait.

As soon as Danae called it quits and headed home, he was going to make good use of the window he'd freed that morning and grab the box of paperwork from the time surrounding Ophelia's death. He'd get it back in place long before work time, and Danae would never be the wiser. He might not have an internet connection in the caretaker's cabin, but he'd had the forethought to bring his laptop and a scanner. If he found anything interesting, he would make a copy.

Danae looked at the stack of dusty notebooks and sighed. "So that's everything from the dresser and nightstands, right?"

"Yeah, but I think there's more under the bed, and I didn't have the heart to even peek into the closet."

She glanced at her watch. "No wonder. It's six o'clock already. You should have let me know it was so late."

"We were both absorbed, and besides, it's not like my Calais social calendar is bursting at the seams."

"Well, then, let me do something about the social calendar to make up for working you like a slave. Dinner at the café—my treat?"

"You don't have to do that."

"I want to. You've done so much for me today. Besides, I don't like eating alone, and my cupboard is bare."

Zach laughed. "So essentially, you're still working me." He said it in a joking tone, but he could tell that what Danae was really avoiding was going home alone. With her independent nature, she'd never admit it, though.

She smiled. "Then I'll throw in a couple of beers and, if you're really good company, a bowl of banana pudding."

"You had me at *dinner,* but I'm not going to turn down the rest. I had a bowl of banana pudding there last night with Carter and have already decided it should be illegal. Seriously, if I lived here, I'd be fat as a tick."

"Not if I keep working you like a mule. Let's get out of here. It's probably dark already."

She rose from the desk and headed out of the office. Zach watched her as she walked away, momentarily mesmerized by the gentle sway of her hips in snug jeans. After talking with Carter, Danae had gone straight to work, and Zach could tell her protective wall was back in place. He'd pushed all thoughts of their shared kiss to the back of his mind while he worked, concentrating instead on the real reason he was in Calais.

All afternoon, he'd been thinking about getting ahold of that paperwork and wondering what he would find, but the moment Danae asked him to dinner, his fickle thoughts had switched right back to that kiss. He could still feel the heat from her body pressed into his, her lips soft and smooth.

He shook his head and hurried out of the office before she wondered what was holding him up. Stealing paperwork and taking that kiss to the next level were the only two answers he could honestly give, and he was pretty sure she wouldn't like either one.

As he stepped out of the office, he almost collided with Danae. "Sorry," he said as he grabbed her shoulders to avoid slamming into her.

"No, it's my fault," she said as she stepped around him and grabbed the notebooks off the desk in the bedroom. "I want to bring some of the records home with me tonight."

Zach clenched his hands as she tossed the notebooks into the box with records from the period surrounding Ophelia's death and then bent over to lift it.

"Let me get that," he said and hefted the box up in front of his face, afraid his frustration was showing.

He carried the box outside and placed it in her car while she locked up the house. With every step, he tried to come up with another idea. So far, Danae had refused his offers to help go through the paperwork, and he understood that. She was a very guarded person and that paperwork might contain information that was private—things she might not feel comfortable letting others know.

He'd seen how uncomfortable she was telling Carter about the payments to the families who had adopted the girls. Carter, of course, had taken it in without even blinking and had moved straight toward analysis rather than lingering over the emotional impact of her findings. But Zach had seen the flex of his jaw and knew the good sheriff was beyond angry. He was just smart enough to know that his anger would only make Danae feel worse.

Zach had liked Carter from the moment he'd met him, but at that moment, his respect for the man had doubled. If anyone was going to get to the bottom of everything happening in Calais, he had no doubt Carter Trahan would be that person. Which left Zach with two objectives— find the information he came for in the first place and prevent anyone from harming Danae.

"I'll follow you to the café," he said and jumped into his truck.

THE INTRUDER WATCHED from between the blinds of an upstairs window as the heiress and her maintenance boy drove away. From his hiding place in the attic, he'd heard every conversation that had occurred in Purcell's office. When the sheriff arrived, he was tempted to leave the attic and sneak down the servants' stairs off the kitchen to see if he could hear the discussion, but it was too much of a risk.

The house was old and many places creaked, which made it nearly impossible to change location without alerting others that he was there.

Lately, it had gotten much harder to get in and out without detection. He was fortunate he still had the front-door key that he'd stolen years ago, and he'd thought when the first heiress finished out her days in the house he could get back to work.

Now he not only had another meddling woman in his way, but also a nosy contractor who seemed more interested in the woman than repairing the house. But that wasn't even the worst part. The worst part was that the woman had just driven off with a box that probably contained the paperwork he'd been looking for.

He banged his hand on the window, damning the day the woman had come to Calais. First, he'd finish the work he needed to do here today, then he'd pay the heiress a visit at her cabin.

And collect what was his.

Chapter Thirteen

All twenty minutes of the slow, bumpy drive, Zach thought about how he was going to access the records. Sneaking into the empty main house and stealing them was one thing, but he could hardly break into Danae's tiny cabin with her in there. The memory of her nine millimeter was stamped on his mind.

When he parked in front of the café, he was no closer to an answer than he'd been when they left the house.

Several tables were occupied, but the far corner held an empty booth with no one seated nearby. Zach pointed to it and Danae nodded. Unless they were yelling, they wouldn't be overheard. As soon as they took their seats, the waitress walked over, a big smile on her face.

"It's great to see you again," Sonia said to Danae. "I didn't get a chance to thank you this morning for quitting. I really needed my job back and there's only so many available in Calais."

Danae smiled. "I'm glad it worked out for everyone."

"I do have a favor to ask, though. I have some personal business to take care of tomorrow. Is there any way you can cover for me? I know it's Saturday, and I don't want to ruin your weekend, but it's just the midmorning shift, so you wouldn't start until nine. Irene said she can come in early and cover starting at eleven."

"Is Johnny okay with it?"

Zach's pulse sped up a tick and he knew he was holding his breath, waiting for the answer. If Danae was out of her cabin for the morning, that would give him time to get in there and look at some of the documents.

Sonia rolled her eyes. "You know Johnny. He said he doesn't care as long as the food gets out before it gets cold."

Danae nodded. "That sounds about right. Sure, I can do it. I hope it's nothing too serious."

Sonia looked down at the floor for a moment and Zach could see a blush creeping up her neck. "Just some old business that needs to be handled. You know how it is."

"I do. Well, good luck with it."

"Thanks. Can I get you guys something to

eat? Pot roast is the special, and I have to say, Jack's outdone himself. It's fantastic."

Zach nodded and Danae held up two fingers. "Make it two, please?" she said.

"Got it," Sonia said and hurried back to the grill to put in the order.

She'd barely left when one of the men at the table nearest them rose from his chair and sauntered over.

Danae looked up and smiled. "Hi, Mr. Martin."

"Roger, please," he said to Danae and then stuck his hand out to Zach. "Roger Martin."

Zach shook the man's hand, wondering what he wanted. His companions, two older men, watched from their table, and Zach could see them speaking to each other, their shoulders almost touching.

"Zach Sargent. It's nice to meet you."

"I don't think I've seen you around before. You a relative?"

Zach shook his head. "I'm a contractor. Mr. Duhon hired me to make some repairs at the LeBeau estate."

"I heard the place was in a real state of disrepair. No way Amos could have kept all that up at his age." Roger turned to Danae, studying her for a moment. "So, I hear you're one of Ophelia's missing daughters."

Danae sat up a bit straighter, clearly uncomfortable under Roger's scrutiny. "I guess it seems strange to everyone that I never said anything."

"Not to me. Purcell wasn't well liked and you couldn't have known what you might walk into here. I don't blame you for taking in the lay of the land before offering up that bit of information."

Zach saw Danae relax a bit.

"Well," Danae said, "I hope others share your feelings."

"I'm sure most do. Anyway, I wanted to apologize for not recognizing you. You were just a baby when I saw you last and you don't look much like your mother...."

"No, I don't. Did you know my mother well?"

Roger nodded. "I was the sheriff for thirty years. I knew everyone. Of course, no one saw her much after she married Purcell. He was a bit of an odd duck. Kept you all locked in that house like the apocalypse was coming."

"That's what I hear. I don't really remember anything."

"No, I guess you wouldn't. She was a nice woman, your mother. What my mother would have called a real lady. Anyway, I just wanted to say that if you need anything, I'm happy to help."

"Thank you."

Roger gave Zach a nod then walked back to his table.

"That was weird," Danae said, glancing back at Roger before turning back to face Zach.

"I take it you weren't friendly before?" Zach asked.

"I was as friendly as I am to all the customers, but I never got to know him like some of the other residents. Until now, he's never spoken to me other than to give his order. I didn't even know he was once the sheriff."

Zach glanced across the café and saw Roger frowning at Danae, his brow scrunched as if in thought. "I wonder what he wanted."

"You got that feeling, too?"

"That he had an ulterior motive for the conversation—sure."

She sighed. "Me, too, but I have no idea what."

"Maybe he just wants some gossip to spread around," Zach said. "I'm guessing there's not a whole lot to talk about in Calais."

"You may be right. The two men with him are both widowers and worse gossips than most women I've known. Roger isn't married now, but I suppose he could have been married before. Maybe they're just bored."

"Or maybe he was looking to hook up with an heiress," Zach teased.

Danae stared at him, her dismay so obvious, he laughed.

"That's just wrong," she said. "He's old enough to be my father."

"A lot of women see that as a plus."

"Weak, lazy women who have daddy issues. I hardly need a man to take care of me." She stopped speaking abruptly and stared at him for a moment. "You're picking on me, and I totally took the bait."

"Sorry, but I couldn't resist, especially as I can't imagine you hooking up with a man for any reason other than you wanted to." Before he could stop himself, his thoughts tumbled out of his mouth. "You're an admirable woman, Danae. I wouldn't blame a man, regardless of age, for taking a shot at you."

She shifted in her seat, looking both flattered and uncomfortable. "Thank you, but I've been surrounded by bulletproof glass for a long time. Anyone shooting at me wouldn't stand a chance."

"Maybe," he said and smiled. What she said was probably true of her past, but he'd already put a crack in that shield. Danae wasn't as insulated as she wanted to believe. Her statement also made him wonder what had happened in her past that made her so cagey, so protective.

"Can I ask you a personal question?" he asked.

"Sure, but I reserve the right not to answer it and to rescind my offer to pay for dinner."

"I'll take my chances." He studied her for a moment, trying to decide the best way to approach the subject, then finally just blurted it out. "What happened to make you so closed off? You don't strike me as a woman who would take abuse, but I figure it had to be something horrible. What did he do—cheat on you? Steal your money?"

Danae's eyes widened. Clearly, the question had been an unexpected one. "I've never been married or even in a serious relationship."

"That surprises me."

"Why?"

"You're a beautiful woman. I can't imagine you don't know that or that other men haven't noticed. You mentioned working in bars and cafés—how many times do you get hit on in a week?"

"That doesn't count. That's just men behaving like boys."

"Yes, but men don't behave like boys unless they think a woman is attractive, something I'm sure you've seen played out a thousand times in your lines of work."

She shrugged and looked down at the table.

"So what caused you to close off this way?" he asked. "You're an intelligent, beautiful, engaging woman, but you've made yourself an island surrounded by suspicion and distrust."

She looked back up at him, but her gaze seemed to go right through him. Whatever haunted Danae LeBeau went much deeper than a failed romance or the betrayal of a friend. Finally, her vision sharpened and she narrowed her eyes at him.

"My choices are not up for discussion," she said.

Before he could reply, Sonia slid two plates of food in front of them. "Y'all need anything else?"

Zach waited a second for Danae to reply, but when she remained silent, he looked up at the smiling waitress and shook his head. "No, thank you."

"Okay. Holler if you do." She jaunted off across the café, leaving them wrapped in silence so thick he could cut it.

DANAE JUMPED INTO her car in front of the café, barely lifting her hand to Zach as he pulled away in his truck. They'd finished the meal in silence except for the barest of sentences, like "Please pass the salt." She knew Zach was disappointed that she wouldn't engage in any of the topics he'd put forward, but she simply wasn't ready.

Yes, she was attracted to him—how could she not be? He was strong, sexy and hell-bent on protecting her. And even though the last thing she needed was a white knight, her heart beat a little bit stronger just knowing that such a man wanted to be her savior.

Then there was the kiss.

She'd been kissed before—probably not as much as people thought, but certainly, she was no innocent maiden. But something about Zach's kisses was different. Her whole body responded to him, every single square inch as if it were awakening for the first time. It was exhilarating and frightening all at the same time.

Then he'd asked her why she didn't let people in, and all romantic thoughts had flown out the window. Her gut had involuntarily clenched as every horrible moment from her past ran through her mind on speed play. Then, for a millisecond, she thought about telling Zach everything.

A second later, the thought fled as if on fire and she returned to her good senses, wondering what in the world had gotten into her. Sure, Zach was gorgeous and she'd be lying if she said she wasn't interested in a physical relationship, but she'd always guarded her past like Fort Knox, intending for it to go to the grave along with her. What in the world had caused her to think, even for a split second, that she should share her past with a man who was essentially a stranger?

Sighing, she rolled down the window to let the cool autumn breeze waft over her. Maybe the air would clear her head. As she put the car in Drive, a hand clutched her shoulder and she jumped.

"Sorry." Amos, the ancient LeBeau estate caretaker, stood outside her car door, leaning on a crutch with his free hand, the other crutch tucked under his arm.

"Amos! You shouldn't be walking around like this. It can't possibly be good for your foot."

He waved a hand in dismissal. "If I have to rest another minute, I'm going to just go ahead and die. My niece is one of those hoverers. Darn woman spends all day standing over me or peeking at me around corners. A man needs some room for his thoughts. Ain't had a single one of my own since I moved in with her."

Danae held in a smile at the crotchety man's delivery. She knew the niece and didn't doubt for a minute that she was hovering—she was decidedly that kind of woman—but she also knew Amos probably made the worst patient ever.

"Anyway," he continued, "I saw your car here from her living-room window, and I've been waiting for her to take her nightly bath so I could sneak out and talk to you. You got a minute for a foolish old man?"

"Of course."

Amos scooted away from the door so that Danae could exit the car, then he pointed to a park bench on the sidewalk in front of the café. She took his arm and guided him over to it, then sat beside him.

"I guess you heard the gossip," she said.

Amos nodded. "I should have figured it out before. I felt something—a connection, I guess—with you the first time I saw you at the café. But I didn't understand why. I mean, you're a nice girl and a pretty one, but it was something more than that."

"I was only a baby when Purcell sent me away, and I don't look like either of my parents, not enough to call attention. It's not surprising that you didn't recognize me. Alaina didn't, either."

"You got her smile—your mom's, that is. Did even when you was a baby. You used to follow me all around the house when I was trying to do my work. If I ignored you, you'd clutch my leg and I'd go dragging you down the hall, you riding my leg and giggling so hard it gave you the hiccups."

Danae smiled. "I wish I could remember that."

"Maybe you will someday. I know you was

just a little thing, but being here, in the house, you might get a flash of memory now and then."

Amos sat up a little straighter and rubbed his old blue jeans with one hand. "You're staying at the house, right?"

"No. I'm still living in my rental. It's on estate property and William said that was good enough to satisfy the requirements of the will."

The relief on the old caretaker's face was apparent. "That's good. I don't like the idea of you being in that house."

"I am there during the day, though. William hired me to go through paperwork for the estate, but I'm not alone. The contractor William hired is there with me."

"I guess that's all right, then." But he didn't look convinced.

"Is there any reason you don't want me to be there?"

Amos stared at the sidewalk and nodded. "I haven't told no one. They'll all think it's just the ramblings of an old man, but I know what happened."

"What happened when?"

"When I broke my foot."

"I thought you fell down the stairs. That's what William said."

"Because that's what I told everyone, but the truth is, I ain't walked up them stairs in ten years or better. Sometimes went a month or more without seeing your stepfather. Hadn't seen him in months when I found him dead on the floor right there in the entry."

Her mind immediately created a visual image of Purcell's cold, lifeless body splayed across the marble floor of the entry, and she crossed her arms over her chest, suddenly feeling a chill.

"So how *did* you break your foot?"

"I was leaving the house by the back door, like I always do. It was still daylight, so I could see clearly. I stepped outside and fumbled a bit for my keys. When I started to turn around to lock the door, someone shoved me."

Danae sucked in a breath.

"Hit both my shoulders like a freight train," Amos continued. "I took a step back, trying to get my balance, but he'd hit me too hard. I twisted my ankle on the way down, then banged it pretty good on the stone patio."

"Who shoved you? Why didn't you call the police?"

"Because no one would have believed me."

"Why not? You were turning around. You had a clear view of your attacker."

Amos shook his head, his eyes wide. "Wasn't no one there."

"I don't understand. You said someone pushed you..."

"Yep, and that's the God's honest truth. Felt his fingers pushing into the tops of my shoulders, but couldn't see a thing."

She sucked in a breath. "You're saying a ghost pushed you?"

"I know what it sounds like, which is why I lied. But I don't want to lie to Ophelia's girls, and I don't want any of you in danger in that house."

"And you think we're in danger?"

Amos nodded. "Your stepfather was a nasty man. I ain't got no proof of it, but I'd dare and say he was evil. I stuck around all those years because I knew one day you and your sisters would return. I knew it in my heart. But after your mother passed, things felt different. Heavy, like something was constantly pressing down on me, trying to smother me."

Danae nodded. "It's an oppressive atmosphere."

"Exactly. Your stepfather never liked you girls. Never liked anyone being in the house unless it couldn't be helped and took darn near an act of God to get him out of it."

She stared at him. "You think my stepfather is haunting the house?"

"I know it sounds crazy, but I don't think he's ever left. That feeling I always got when I was alone in the house with him is still there. And I could swear I smelled Wild Turkey when I fell. He was always drinking Wild Turkey. I haven't been able to stand the smell for over twenty years."

Danae took a deep breath and blew it slowly out, trying to make sense of what the caretaker said. His expression—half earnest, half afraid—told her that he believed every word he'd said. But was his aging mind playing tricks on him?

"Why would my stepfather haunt the house?"

Amos shook his head. "My granny used to say that your spirit only stuck around on this earth if your body died and your soul was vexed."

"Like if someone was in a highly emotional state or a crisis?"

"Yep."

"But that doesn't make sense for Purcell. He had a mansion to live in and didn't have to work. What could be keeping him here?"

"Anger."

She stared at Amos, the conversation with Carter playing back in her mind. "Carter found out Purcell didn't have free access to the estate money—just an allowance and the ability to buy assets of approved value. Carter thinks he was buying stuff and then selling it for the cash."

Amos nodded. "That very well could be. Whenever he'd show himself, he was usually grumbling about being stuck in the house. I always thought it was odd that he stayed as he didn't seem to like anything about it, but if what you say is true, then I guess he couldn't leave."

"Not unless he wanted to support himself, and apparently, he was willing to give up his life to avoid work." She shook her head. "I've known some lazy people in my day, but never anything like that. It doesn't make sense."

Amos narrowed his eyes at her. "It does if he was hiding from someone even worse than him."

The conversation with Amos ran through Danae's mind a hundred times on the drive to her cabin. Carter's cursory check into Purcell's background had yielded almost nothing but maybe he'd find more in New Orleans. Maybe the fingerprints would give them some information about the mysterious man who'd removed her mother from society and given away her children as if they were unwanted pets.

Maybe Amos was right. Maybe Purcell used Ophelia's remote estate to escape a worse fate. When she'd died, he probably thought he would collect an amount of money that allowed him to go to the far reaches of the earth to hide from his past. And when he heard the terms of the will, he got angry.

His escape to Calais became his prison.

Chapter Fourteen

Carter paced the interview room at the New Orleans Police Station, his coffee sitting forgotten and cold on the table. His former captain hadn't even hesitated when Carter had asked him to lift and run the prints, and he'd been astounded when Carter told him about all the trouble going on in the tiny town of Calais.

The captain had warned him the lab was backed up and it might take a while, but Carter didn't have any business in New Orleans other than Purcell and no other leads if the fingerprints didn't provide them. He reached for the coffee and sighed when he felt the cold cup. Maybe he should take a walk around the block—something just to get out of the building.

Just as he made up his mind to leave, the door opened and the captain walked in, carrying a stack of paper. His expression left no doubt that not only had he found something, but that he also didn't like it.

"You've really stepped in the middle of a hornet's nest," the captain said. "Those prints hadn't been loaded five minutes before the computer screen started whirling so fast I was afraid it would fry. I printed it all out and hurried in here before the phone calls start."

Carter stared. "Who was he—D. B. Cooper?"

"Close enough. His real name was Raymond Lambert, and he was a hit man for the Primeaux family. They run a lot of the adult-trade business in New Orleans and dabble a bit in threats and extortion. Got a couple of politicians in their pocket, if you ask me, but I haven't been able to put a case together yet."

Carter slumped onto the table. "You're kidding me. What the hell was a hit man doing in Calais?"

"My guess is he was hiding. Says here that word on the street was old man Primeaux put a price on his head, but no one has ever heard why. Lambert simply disappeared twenty-five years ago and everyone figured someone from the Primeaux family had caught up with him."

"That definitely fits with what little I know about the man. Everyone assumed he was agoraphobic, but maybe he was just lying low to avoid the risk of being identified."

"Seems an odd choice to make for a man in his mid-forties, but some people will do almost anything to avoid an honest day's work. He probably figured he could eventually talk the widow into leaving Louisiana."

"Probably," Carter agreed. "The police didn't look into his disappearance?"

"Of course—we're cops. But you know how those families operate. They close ranks and you can't get anyone talking, not even about each other."

"So he left New Orleans and became Trenton Purcell and romanced a young widow for her fortune."

"Looks like. What I don't understand is, why didn't he leave Calais after the widow died?"

"I can answer that one," Carter said and gave the captain a rundown of the terms of the estate.

When he finished, the captain whistled. "I bet he was madder than a hornet. Probably thought he'd won the lottery when she passed so young, and then finds out he's tied to those four walls in the middle of the swamp unless he wants to leave with the shirt on his back. That probably didn't do anything to improve his disposition."

"He was a nasty man. The more I find out about him, the more I wish he was still alive so that I could throttle him myself."

The captain nodded. "There's a name in the file—an FBI agent who was working up a case against the family about the time Lambert disappeared. He's retired now, but still lives in New Orleans. I wrote his name and phone number on the top of the printout. Thought if you had time, you might want to talk to him."

Carter took the printout from the captain and glanced at the name and telephone number penciled on the top sheet. "Yeah, that would be great."

The captain extended his hand to Carter. "It was good seeing you, Trahan. If you ever change your mind about coming back to the force, I'd be happy to have you."

Carter shook his hand and nodded. "Thanks, sir, but I think Calais is where I belong."

The captain shook his head. "Seems your attempt to move to a simpler place has failed you all the way around."

"Seems like," Carter agreed. "But I'm going to fix that."

DANAE STUCK HER HAND out of the shower and reached for the towel hanging on the hook next to it. The hot water had done wonders for her neck and back, both of which had grown increasingly tighter as the day had worn on, culminating with all-out knots after her conversation with Amos.

She dried off her body then wrapped the towel around her head before stepping out of the tub to grab the shorts and T-shirt she'd draped across the vanity. A draft of chilly night air wafted through the bathroom and she quickly pulled the clothes on. The days were still warm and humid, but the temperatures dropped at night, especially in the swamp.

As she reached for her hairbrush, she heard the floor creak at the front of the cabin. Immediately, she froze, trying to lock in on the noise. Then it came again, the faintest creak of the floorboards.

Someone was in the cabin with her.

Mentally cursing herself for leaving her pistol in her purse, she scanned the bathroom for anything that made a viable weapon and grabbed the scissors from the vanity. She inched over to the bathroom door and eased it open, praying that the hinges didn't squeak. When the door was open enough for her to edge through it, she peered down the hall toward the living room, but couldn't see anything moving.

The sounds of the swamp were the only things that broke the still night air, and she wondered if the intruder had gone. Or maybe she'd been wrong and no one had ever been inside with her. Maybe the stress of her situation and her overworked imagination were getting the best of her.

She eased down the hall toward the living

room, clutching the scissors and praying she'd blown the entire thing out of proportion. When she reached the opening to the living room, she scanned the room as much as possible without stepping into it, but nothing appeared out of place.

You're an idiot.

Shaking her head, she stepped from the hallway into the living room, and that was when he sprang. In an instant, he grabbed her shoulder with one hand and wrapped his arm around her neck, pulling it so tightly she couldn't breathe.

Before her mind could even process what was happening, instinct kicked in and she stabbed his arm with the scissors. He let out a roar and released her, shoving her into the hallway as he ran for the door.

She stumbled backward, barely managing not to fall, then rushed back into the living room as the intruder yanked open the front door. She lunged for the kitchen table and grabbed her purse, pulling her pistol from inside. Before she could get off a round, the intruder dashed out the front door.

She ran across the room and scanned the front of the cabin, but couldn't see anything in the inky blackness. Still clutching her pistol, she slammed the door and locked it, then grabbed her cell phone and started to dial Carter when she remembered he was in New Orleans. Cursing, she punched in Zach's number, praying that the connection was strong enough on both ends for the call to go through.

It was all she could do to keep from crying out in relief when he answered on the second ring.

"There was someone in my cabin," she blurted out before he even finished his greeting. "I heard something when I got out of the shower and I thought I'd imagined it, but then he grabbed me and I stabbed him with my scissors. Then he ran and I grabbed my gun, but it was too late. He disappeared into the swamp before I could fire."

Her breath came out in a giant whoosh and she realized she'd been holding it through the entire delivery.

"Are you all right?" Zach's voice sounded as panicked as she felt. "I'm on my way. Lock the doors and don't you dare put down that gun. I'll be there in a couple of minutes."

"Don't hang up, okay?"

"I won't."

Danae hurried to the corner of the living room opposite the door and sank down into a squatting position next to the couch. This way, she had the advantage over anyone entering the room. A quick scan of the living room and kitchen revealed no broken glass, and she was certain she'd drawn the dead bolt on the front door as soon as she'd entered the cabin. Clearly he hadn't entered that way, but it didn't look as if he'd come through a window, either, so where had he gained access?

Part of her wanted to get up and look for the point of entry, but the other part wanted everything to do with self-preservation and nothing to do with things that could wait until Zach arrived.

"Are you still there?" she asked.

"Yeah, I'm in my truck, but I'm going to have to put the phone down. I need both hands to negotiate the roads at high speed."

"Okay," she said and clutched the phone even tighter. She could hear Zach's truck engine and silently willed it to move faster, but she knew speed was next to impossible on the winding, bumpy roads.

A second later, her phone beeped once then went silent.

"No!" She looked at the display, but service had dropped to nothing.

Surely he was almost there. It had been several minutes since she'd called, right? It felt like longer than that, so he had to be close.

Breathe.

Realizing that she was beginning to panic,

she took a deep breath and slowly blew it out. Never had she felt so vulnerable, so completely exposed, as she did right now, and it was a feeling she didn't know how to handle.

The crunch of gravel had her springing up from her hiding place, and she ran to the window to peek outside. Relief flooded her when she saw Zach jump out of his truck and run for the door. She managed to get it open just as he arrived and he rushed inside, then clutched her shoulders, looking her up and down.

"Are you hurt?" he asked.

The worry and care in his voice and expression were so clear that it made her heart ache. She shook her head, afraid to speak, and a single sob escaped. Instantly, he drew her into his arms and held her close to him, running his hand down her hair and whispering in her ear that she was safe.

She clutched him, her arms clenched around his strong back, and buried her head in his shoulder, crying openly and afraid she'd never be able to let him go.

Finally, the last tear ran down her cheek and her breathing began to return to normal. She pushed herself back enough to look at him.

"I'm sorry—" she began.

"Don't you dare apologize," he said. "Someone attacked you in your home. Anyone would have been terrified."

"I was," she said and looked down, almost embarrassed that she'd been so scared.

He placed his finger under her chin and tilted her head back up until she met his gaze. "But you fought back and got away," he said. "You're a strong, brave woman."

Her heart pounded in her throat, and more than anything, she wanted him to kiss her. No matter how hard she'd tried to resist her attraction to Zach, her body always betrayed her. It came alive when he was close to her, in a way she'd never felt before. Her heart beat stronger, her skin was more sensitive and her head felt as if she were walking on the moon.

She felt her body lean forward, anticipating the kiss, but instead, he released her and scanned the cabin.

"How did he get in?" he asked.

Her mind leaped back to reality and she realized they could be at risk standing here.

"I don't know," she said, her fear returning. "I started to look around after I called you but then I thought it was smarter to remain stationary with a clear view of all entry points."

He smiled. "Definitely smarter. Most people wouldn't have thought of it. Let's check the cabin."

She nodded. "There's not much to it, so that's an advantage. I drew the dead bolt on the front door as soon as I walked inside, so he didn't get in that way."

He scanned the floors in the kitchen and living room. "I don't see any glass, but let's check the windows. I'm sure you keep them locked, right?"

"You know it," she said as she moved to check the window on the far wall as Zach checked the front living-room window.

"All locked tight," he said and moved into the kitchen to check the small window over the sink. "This one, too."

They walked down the hall and checked the two bedroom windows but they were locked tight.

"I don't understand," Danae said. "The bathroom window is no more than a vent slot. Only a very small child could fit through there and they'd have to have a ladder to reach it. So how did he get in?"

Zach frowned. "My guess is through the front door."

She sucked in a breath. "He was already inside when I got home. I literally locked him inside with me. How many keys to LeBeau property are walking around this town?"

She dropped down onto the edge of the bed,

her mind racing with all the possibilities of what could have happened. "But that makes no sense. When I got home, I headed straight for the shower. He could have attacked me then and there's no way I could have defended myself."

"I know, which leaves us with two possibilities—either he was trying to scare you or you aren't what he was here for."

"But what else is there? This cabin doesn't hold the collectibles that the main house does. Every stitch of furniture and decor in this place probably wouldn't bring a hundred dollars at a garage sale."

"Maybe he thinks you have something valuable."

"A café waitress? Not likely."

"An heiress," he corrected. "Far more likely."

She shook her head. "Not yet. Everyone in town knows we haven't inherited yet. There's no reason for them to expect I have anything of more value than I came to town with, and I haven't had any trouble until now."

"Maybe he thinks you took something of value from the house."

She frowned. "I suppose that's possible, but all I took was paperwork. The paperwork!"

She jumped up from the bed and ran into the kitchen, but the box of paperwork still sat next to the dining table.

"Is it all there?" Zach asked.

She reached into the box and pulled out a stack of paper. "It looks like it, but I thought I put those notebooks you took from Purcell's bedroom on top. Now they're wedged below some other papers."

"Maybe he was going through the paperwork while you were in the shower and wasn't able to find what he was looking for before you finished. When you came down the hall, he couldn't get out in time, so he attacked you instead."

Her heart began to pound in her temples. "He was inside the main house today. That's the only way he could know I took the paperwork home with me."

Zach nodded. "That's what Carter and I believe."

"We're going to have to watch everything we say—whisper or go into our cars to talk—but I refuse to stop my investigation. I must be onto something if he's willing to risk coming inside my cabin. If I'd been able to get my pistol in time, I would have shot him without hesitation."

"I know you would have. It's one of the things I like best about you."

Despite the seriousness of the situation, the unexpected comment made her smile. "So what now? Carter won't be back until tomorrow, and

I don't see the point in calling this in. He was wearing gloves, and I haven't found the scissors, so I have to assume he took them with him. He didn't even stick around long enough to leave a speck of blood."

"We'll tell Carter tomorrow when he gets back. In the meantime, pack up some clothes. You can stay with me in the caretaker's cabin."

"No." Her reaction was instant. "Surely he's not stupid enough to come back here tonight."

"I'm not going to bet on it. The caretaker's cabin is basically one big room and a bathroom. It's even easier to secure than this place, plus I have some spare locks that I can use to change the ones on your place and the house tomorrow."

"You carry around spare locks?"

"Contractor, remember? I do a lot of rehab work. The last thing I want is equipment walking away in the middle of the night because I was foolish enough to leave the old locks in place."

Tired, frustrated and knowing she didn't have a good argument to the contrary, she rose from the bed and pulled a backpack out of the tiny closet.

"Give me a minute to pack," she said. "And I want to bring the paperwork with us. If that's what he's after, then the last thing I want to do is make it easy on him."

Chapter Fifteen

Zach pushed open the door to the caretaker's cabin with one hand and clutched his shotgun with the other. It only took him a minute to ensure the cabin was empty, then he hurried back to his truck to open the door for Danae.

"Go ahead inside," he said. "I'll grab the box."

She jumped out of the truck, hesitating long enough to scan the swamp on each side of the cabin, then hustled inside. He grabbed the box from the backseat and followed close behind her.

She stood in the middle of the small room, clutching her backpack and looking extremely uneasy.

"There's only the pullout sofa," he said as he placed the box on the kitchen counter. "Amos gives *minimalist living* a whole new definition, but I can take the recliner. It appears to be the one thing the man splurged on."

"I can't ask you to give up your bed."

"Who said you are? Make yourself comfortable…if that's possible. Are you hungry?"

"No," she said as she dropped her backpack on the floor and sank onto the couch "My stomach's kind of in a knot."

"A drink, then." He grabbed a couple of glasses from the cabinet and poured them both half-full with scotch.

"A happy client gave this to me," he said as he handed her the glass and took a seat beside her. "I'm normally a beer guy, but I have to admit, this is really smooth."

She took a sip and nodded. "I've bartended long enough to know this is expensive. He must have been really happy."

Zach took a sip and nodded. "Happy and loaded. I figured it wasn't cheap as he took it out of his own collection, but I've been afraid to look it up. I figure I'll never be able to afford another bottle."

She took another drink and stared straight ahead, and for a moment, he wondered if she'd even heard a word he'd just said.

"She was an addict," Danae said quietly. "Rose—the woman who took me in. It started with alcohol, but eventually, it wasn't enough."

He froze, wavering between being thrilled that Danae was finally talking to him and wanting to express outrage at what she'd just said.

"I'm sorry," he said, deciding keeping it simple was best. "I can't imagine how difficult it must have been for you."

"Awful, horrible, terrible… All those words put together aren't enough to describe it. *Living hell* may be as close as I could come."

She took a deep breath and blew it out. Wisely, he kept silent, afraid that if he asked a question, she would stop talking.

"We had a house at first," she continued. "A shack, really, about this size, but it had four walls and a good roof, and we were happy there. Until we weren't. With her issues, Rose didn't hold jobs for very long, but she managed okay when it was just alcohol. When I hit junior high, she tried cocaine, and later, heroin."

Her eyes grew misty and he slid closer to her, taking her hand in his and giving it a squeeze.

"I wasn't really surprised when we lost the house. The landlord had been more than understanding, but he had bills to pay, as well. We lived at a shelter for a while, but when they caught Rose using, they kicked us out. For a while we lived in her car. Then she met some guy at the truck stop she was waitressing at, and we moved in with him. I think she'd known him less than a week."

"That's so dangerous," he said.

Danae nodded. "It was—is—but that didn't

stop Rose. The worst part is, I can't even tell you his name. He was the first of many men that Rose used for shelter and money. The fix was really all she cared about."

"Was she physically abusive?"

"Not often, but it happened. Usually, she wasn't mean when she was high or drunk. She was just…I don't know—checked out, I guess. I don't think Rose's childhood was all that great. I always figured she was hiding from her past with a bottle or a needle."

"She should never have taken you in, knowing she had problems."

"I'm sure she did it for the money. Twenty thousand dollars probably covered Rose's meager expenses and alcohol for years. She never cared anything about having me around, except to wait on her and clean house, but she was only physically abusive a couple of times. The men were another story."

Zach felt his back tighten. "Did they…?" He clenched his free hand into a fist, unable to even finish the question.

"No, nothing like that."

Relief coursed through him so strong it made him dizzy. "Thank God."

"But that's the direction it was going. Once I turned thirteen and started to develop, I saw the way they looked at me. Even then, I understood what it meant and how wrong it was. I also knew that not only would Rose not be strong enough to defend me, but that for the right offer at the right time, she may even sell me. So I left when I was fifteen."

"And went where?"

"A rent-by-the week motel far enough away from Rose that she wouldn't find me. I'd been hustling on the street for a while. Nothing illegal—at least, not that I'm aware of. Mostly delivery for local businesses. I was cheaper than delivery services or gas and parking fees."

Zach stared, trying to wrap his mind around a fifteen-year-old girl managing on her own. "What kind of motel rents a room to a minor?"

"Probably any in that area of town, but I had ID that said I was eighteen. That's the only illegal thing I've ever done. There was a guy who lived down the block from one of Rose's many shack-ups. He dealt in fake IDs, social security cards, that sort of thing."

Suddenly, something that Zach had wondered about fell into place. "That's how you were able to come here under an assumed name and not raise any questions. You had identification."

She gave him a questioning look.

"Carter told me," he explained. "Jack scowled at him a couple of times and I asked about it. He brought me up to speed on the local gossip."

"Before I came to Calais, I wandered around from town to town, but nothing ever felt right. I met some nice people, but I didn't get close to anyone. I couldn't afford to when I was a minor. I was afraid I'd be put into the system. I'd met street kids who'd been in the system and it didn't sound any better than living with Rose."

She sighed. "It was self-preservation at first, but I guess it became habit. Not that it didn't prevent me from making some mistakes. I trusted the wrong people a time or two and quickly learned my lesson. A lot of people are not anything like what they appear. My distance allowed me the time to see them for who they truly were."

"And in all that time, no man ever passed your assessment?"

"No." She looked over at him. "I mean, I've been with other men... I'm not... It just didn't go anywhere. No matter how sincere they appeared, I couldn't trust them. Then I came to Calais and everything felt different. Maybe I was simply tired of living a shadow of a life."

"Maybe it's because Calais is where you belong."

"Do you really think so?"

The hope in her expression as she looked at him made his heart break for the lost little girl who had spent a lifetime looking for her place in the world.

"Yes, I do. Everyone here seems to like you. I haven't met your sister, but I like Carter, and he doesn't seem like the kind of man who would settle down with a questionable woman. So I'll go out on a limb and say that Alaina is probably a good person and happy you're here."

Her eyes misted up and she nodded. "Alaina is a great person—one of the best I've ever met. I felt a connection with her immediately. She's worried about me, and I can tell it's real because it feels so strange. Nice strange, if that makes sense."

"It does. Danae, you're a wonderful woman who's overcome a past that most people would have crumbled under. I know it's not in your nature to let people in, but your life would become so much more if you took that risk. Sometimes it comes with great heartache, but without risking heartache, you can't experience great joy."

She sniffed and gave him a small smile. "How did a contractor get so philosophical?"

"My dad was a funeral director, and my mom died when I was five. I learned about the fragility of life at a young age. All of us have only so much time on this earth, and none of us know how much time that is."

"So I should live life as if it were my last day?"

"Well, maybe not your last day, but perhaps second-to-last?"

She laughed softly as she stared at him, her amber eyes looking so deeply into his that he wondered if she could read his mind. He hoped not, because at the moment, his thoughts were anything but pure.

She was so beautiful—the fine bone structure of her face, her full lips and glossy black hair. Sitting on a broken-down couch, wearing shorts and a T-shirt, she was the most gorgeous woman he'd ever seen.

"Maybe I'll start living that second-to-last day now," she whispered and leaned over, brushing her lips against his.

He told himself it was a bad idea—to take when she was so vulnerable—but nothing could have stopped him from responding. Danae had awakened parts of him that he'd never known were there. She'd already taken his heart and soul. The only thing left to give was his physical self, and he'd been fighting that urge for too long.

He wrapped his arms around her and deepened the kiss. She ran her hands up his back, and immediately, he wanted her hands everywhere—his hands everywhere. He lowered his mouth to kiss the nape of her neck and she groaned, leaning her head back so that he could trail kisses across her chest.

He slipped one hand under her T-shirt and found her bare breast, giving silent thanks that she'd dressed in haste and left off the bra. Her smooth skin sent his body into overdrive, and he decided there was entirely too much cloth between them.

With a single flourish, he pulled her shirt over her head and dropped it on the floor. When he took her full breast into his mouth, she trembled and tugged at his shirt.

"I want you now," she whispered.

No more prompting needed, he rose and pulled off his clothes, then snagged a condom from his wallet. Danae pulled off her shorts and he pushed her gently back on the couch before rising above her.

In one fluid motion, he entered her and gasped.

She clutched his back and he kissed her again, then set the pace that quickly sent both of them over the edge.

CARTER PULLED INTO Calais around 2:00 a.m. He'd originally planned to stay the night in New Orleans, but his day had revealed so much information, he knew he'd be too restless to sleep for a long while. Finally deciding there was no use paying for a hotel room when he wasn't going to use the bed for hours, he jumped into his truck and headed back home. His bed there was more comfortable and free, and this way, he'd be able to talk to Danae first thing in the morning.

He debated between a shower or food—it had been a long time since he'd had either—but food finally won out and he fixed a sandwich and ate it standing over the sink. If Alaina were there, she'd fuss at him for the bachelor behavior and he smiled thinking about it. He missed his fiancée, more than he'd ever thought possible. She'd slipped so easily into his life, making it complete when he hadn't even realized something was missing.

A few minutes later the hot spray and shower steam relaxed his muscles, which had tightened during the seemingly never-ending drive on the lonely highways from New Orleans to Calais. It had been a really long but productive day, and he was glad he'd finally gotten to the bottom of the odd habits of Trenton Purcell, aka Raymond Lambert. He couldn't wait to tell his mother, who'd always loathed the man, that her instincts were right, as always.

He was almost waterlogged when he heard his cell phone ringing. Frowning, he jumped out of the shower, grabbing a towel as he hurried into the kitchen to grab his phone. He'd notified dispatch when he was on his way back to Calais, but tomorrow was his day off, and the deputy he'd hired a couple weeks before was on call.

The display showed the sheriff's department number, and he felt his heart rate tick up a beat as he answered. Something was seriously wrong for them to call at this hour.

"I'm sorry to call you in the middle of the night," said Margaret, the night dispatcher, "but we've got a bad situation at Jack Granger's place."

Carter clenched the phone, praying that the cook hadn't gotten drunk and done something incredibly stupid. He'd never been brought up for domestic violence before, but he was a mean drunk and had been a pressure cooker of emotion lately.

"What did he do?" Carter asked.

"He was murdered."

Involuntarily, his jaw dropped, and for a moment, his mind went completely blank. "Come again?"

"He was murdered. The deputy's on the scene, but he's panicking."

"You think?" Ten days on the job in a town that usually boasted drunk-driving citations, poaching and the occasional bar brawl, and the completely green twenty-two-year-old had been called to a murder scene in the middle of the night.

"Give me a second to throw on clothes. I'll call you from the road and you can fill me in on what you know."

He tossed the phone onto the kitchen table and ran into the bedroom to throw on jeans, tennis shoes and a T-shirt. Not even taking time to run a brush through his wet hair, he strapped on his pistol, grabbed his phone and ran out the door and into his truck. He dialed dispatch as soon as he pulled out of the driveway.

"What do you know?" he asked, wanting to get as much information as possible before he walked onto the scene.

"His girlfriend, Cherise, was out of town with the kids, helping her sister, who'd just had surgery. She called that evening for Jack, but he never answered and no one at the café had seen him since he left work. She waited awhile, but by ten o'clock, decided something might be wrong and headed back here to check."

"Please tell me she didn't have the kids with her."

"She was smart enough to leave them sleeping at her sister's, and it's a good thing. Deputy Finley said he'd been stabbed repeatedly—*hacked* was the word he used. He sounded like he was going to pass out when he called in. I figured Cherise was in even worse condition than the deputy, so I called Doc Broussard while I was waiting on you to call back. He's on his way."

"Good." Carter would need the doctor not only to calm Cherise, but also to give him an idea on time of death and weapon. Doc Broussard wasn't well versed in forensics, but he'd seen enough knife wounds that he might be able to give them an idea what weapon was used.

"Is there anything else I can do?" Margaret asked.

"Yeah, call my mom. Give her a rundown of the situation and tell her to prepare a room for Cherise. She'll need a place to rest and someone to keep watch over her for a bit."

"I'll do it as soon as I hang up with you."

Several seconds of silence followed, and for a moment, he thought they'd been disconnected.

Then Margaret's voice came through again, and this time, he could hear the fear in her voice.

"Carter, what's going on in this town?"

"I don't know, but I'm going to find out."

Chapter Sixteen

Danae handed Zach a refill of coffee as he sat on a stool in front of her cabin door, changing out the locks. As usual, she'd awakened early, but for the first time in her life, she hadn't awakened alone. Wrapped in Zach's arms, even the lumpy old pullout couch felt like the bed in a five-star hotel.

She'd snuggled against him and felt him stir, lower parts first, then working upward. They'd made love again, this time slow and easy, with him taking the time to enjoy every curve of her body. She'd languished in the attention and the way her body responded to his touch.

Before the sun even peeked over the cypress trees, they'd eaten breakfast, and Zach had changed the locks on the caretaker's cabin before they'd headed back to her cabin to do the same.

In the bright daylight, the cabin looked so innocent, so free of trouble, but the previous night was so clear in her mind, the attack might as well have happened five minutes ago. Still clutching her coffee mug, she crossed her arms as the cool morning air wafted inside the cabin and ran across her bare skin.

"When should we call Carter?"

Zach placed a screw in the door frame and tightened the lock onto the door. "He said he would head back early this morning. It's almost seven a.m. We can try him now, if you want."

She nodded and stepped into the kitchen to retrieve her cell phone. "If we don't catch him before he leaves New Orleans, we may not be able to for a while. I don't think there's much signal to speak of on the highways in between."

"Probably not."

She pushed in Carter's number and was relieved when he answered on the first ring, although he sounded beat. A flash of guilt passed over her that she'd woken him up when he probably could have used the sleep.

"I'm sorry to wake you," she said.

"You didn't. I haven't been to bed yet."

A million things flashed through her mind, none of them good. "Is Alaina all right?" she asked, getting her most important worry out of the way.

"She's fine. Nothing to do with her, but I need to talk to you."

"Good. I need to talk to you, too."

"I'm about to finish up here. I can be there in about thirty minutes. Are you at the house or your cabin?"

She was momentarily shocked to hear he was back in Calais, which opened up an entirely new avenue of possibilities for his lack of sleep. "I'm at my cabin. So is Zach. We'll wait for you here."

"I'll see you in thirty."

She slipped the phone into her pocket and looked over at Zach, who'd stopped working.

"What's wrong?" he asked.

"I don't know," she said and relayed Carter's whereabouts and lack of sleep to Zach.

His face darkened. "That doesn't sound good."

"I know. I could hear it in his voice. He sounded exhausted, but also frustrated, angry and sad, all rolled into one. What could have happened?"

"Your sister's all right, though?"

She nodded. "If he needs to talk to me, then it's something to do with me, right?"

"Or just the estate in general."

"William handles the estate and I can't think of a legal matter that would keep him up all night."

Zach rose from the stool and wrapped his

arms around her. "There's no use worrying about it now. We'll know everything in thirty minutes."

"You're right. I'm going to take a shower before he gets here. Maybe the steam will help clear my mind."

He kissed her before releasing her.

"I'm almost done with the locks. I'll do another check of the windows while you're showering."

"Thanks," she said and headed for the shower.

She was pulling her hair back into a ponytail when she heard Zach call out that Carter was there. She took a deep breath and headed into the living room, where Carter stood next to Zach.

He looked as if he'd been through hell. His face was drawn and dark circles pooled below his eyes. His posture was stiff and she could see his jaw flexing.

"Do you want something to drink?" she asked. "I put on coffee."

He looked so grateful, she felt sorry for him.

"That would be great," he said.

"Take a seat," she said and waved her hand at the kitchen table. "You look like you're about to keel over."

He slid into one of the chairs and Zach took a

seat across from him as she poured three cups of coffee and carried them to the table.

"I feel like I'm about to keel over. I'm going straight to bed for a couple hours when I leave here, but I had to talk to you first." He took a big sip of the coffee. "You said you had something to tell me?"

Danae slid into the chair next to him. "Yes," she said and filled him in on what had happened the night before, only leaving out the part about her and Zach getting naked.

Carter stiffened as she described the attack and then slammed one hand on the table and cursed. "He could have killed you!"

"Zach and I talked about that," Danae said. "But if he wanted to kill me, he could have when I was in the shower."

Carter shook his head. "Doesn't matter. You came out of the bathroom before he'd finished whatever he was doing. You changed the game, and he had to change accordingly. If you hadn't taken the scissors with you…"

Danae clutched her coffee mug with both hands, just realizing they were shaking.

Carter placed his hand on her arm. "You were smart and it might have saved your life. I don't suppose you can tell me exactly where you stabbed him, can you?"

"I think so." She motioned to Zach. "Can

you stand behind me and put your arm around my neck?"

They stood and Zach did as she'd described.

"I had the scissors in my right hand," she said. "I brought my arm up and stabbed like this." She mimicked the movement.

Carter nodded. "Probably the middle of the forearm."

"Are you going to try to find someone with that injury in Calais?" Zach asked as they took their seats again.

"I might not have to." He blew out a breath and ran one hand through his hair. "Look, I was going to come talk to you even before you called. Something happened last night and I don't want you hearing it around town."

Danae felt her stomach clutch.

"Jack Granger was murdered."

A waved of nausea rolled over her and she put her hands on the table to steady herself as the blood rushed from her head.

"How…? You're sure it was…?"

Carter nodded. "He was stabbed, which is why I asked about the location of the wound on your attacker."

"If you find one on his arm," Zach said, "then you'll know he was the one stalking Danae, right?"

"Not necessarily," Carter said and frowned.

"I don't want to distress you any more than I already have. I know Jack was a friend, of sorts, anyway. Let's just say that he didn't go down without a fight."

Danae gasped, the image of the disgruntled cook fighting to his death rolling through her mind like a horror movie. "Oh, my God. Who found him?"

"His girlfriend, Cherise. She's a bit of a wreck. Doc Broussard gave her something to knock her out and my mom's taking care of her for now."

Danae nodded, trying to force her overwhelmed mind to focus. "That's good. Your mother will know what to do. She always does."

You're rattling.

She clenched her hands and released then clenched again, trying to work out some of her frustration, fear and anger without losing control.

"There's more," Carter said. "We searched his house—standard procedure—and we found a key to the front door of the LeBeau mansion."

"He did errands for Purcell, right?" Danae asked. "So I guess it's not completely shocking that he had a key, although I think William asked him about it a while back and he said he didn't have one."

"That's right," Carter confirmed. "In addition to the key, we found the phone number for the guy who attacked Alaina on a pad of paper in his desk drawer."

She gasped. "You think he helped that man get to Alaina?"

Carter sighed, his expression sad. "I don't want to, but I think Jack was at a place where he would have done anything for money. It wouldn't have taken much for someone to find out his situation and capitalize on it."

"How could he?" Danae asked. "How could he help someone with murder?"

Carter shook his head. "I'd like to think he was told it was just a prank or that Alaina had something her attacker needed to steal. I don't think Jack was so far gone that he'd willingly agree to murder. At least, I don't want to think that."

"But if he attacked me last night…"

"You said yourself that if he wanted to kill you, he could have," Carter pointed out. "The bigger question is, who killed Jack?"

Zach nodded. "Someone who thought he was getting sloppy."

Carter looked Danae straight in the eyes. "I need you to be very careful. Whoever was pulling Jack's strings doesn't have a problem with eliminating anything that stands in his way."

"I WISH YOU wouldn't do this," Zach said as he held open Danae's car door so that she could slip inside.

"I promised I'd work Sonia's shift. Johnny will have to pull double duty after what happened to Jack and he's going to need all the help he can get. Carter will keep it quiet as long as he can, but it's going to make the rounds. By lunchtime, everyone in Calais will start cycling through there to find out what happened."

"Okay. I'll finish nailing the windows shut, and then I'll be right behind you. I'm not letting you out of my sight, even if it means sitting in the café half the day."

He leaned in to kiss her gently on the lips. "Be careful. Keep your cell phone right next to you and call me if anything seems even remotely out of place."

"I will."

He closed the door and stood there watching until her car disappeared into the swamp, then he hustled back inside the cabin and straight to the box of paperwork on the table. He didn't have much time to go through it before he needed to leave for the café, but he had to take advantage of every opportunity, no matter how slight.

The first hundred pages were receipts, and he flipped through them quickly, then tossed them aside. Somewhere in this mess had to be check registers or logs—some detailed list of expenditures.

He'd already seen the ledger with the payments to the families that had taken the sisters. Danae had placed those on the top of the other paperwork and he'd been able to quickly review it while she was showering. But the dates were all wrong. Those payments were made more than a month after Zach's father deposited the lump of cash into his checking account.

Purcell's notebooks.

He reached back into the box and pulled out the notebooks he'd retrieved from Purcell's bedroom.

Pay dirt!

The notebooks contained page after page of descriptions and costs. He flipped through the first notebook, checking the dates, but they were too recent, as were the entries in the second. The third notebook he pulled out of the stack was wavy, as if it had gotten damp then dried, and the edges of the paper had yellowed.

He flipped it open and his pulse ticked up a notch. This one was from the right time period—just before Ophelia's death. Running his finger down the right column, he scanned each amount paid, then turned the page and did it again and again.

On the fifth page, he froze, his finger hovering over a twenty-thousand-dollar entry.

He knew he wasn't breathing when he finally forced himself to look to the left and read the notation. All it contained was a set of initials. D.S.

David Sargent.

The date was five days before his dad made the deposit.

A wave of anger and disgust ran through him and he closed the notebook, then slammed his fist on the table. It was everything he'd been afraid of.

You knew the risk when you came here.

That much was true. He'd known the risks of finding out something about his father that changed the way he viewed the man he'd always held in such high esteem. But even that paled in comparison to the bigger problem.

Telling Danae that he'd lied to her and, even worse, exactly why.

He hadn't expected to fall for her. Initially, he'd pursued her as a form of distraction, but the more he'd been around her, the more he genuinely wanted her. She was beautiful and intelligent, but beneath that strong exterior was a fragile woman who'd never been able to rely on another person. She'd lowered her guard and trusted him. He'd repaid her by lying. More than anything, he wished he could take that part back.

He dropped the notebooks back into the box and hefted the entire thing up to take with him to the café. As soon as Danae got a break, he'd pull out the notebook and explain everything to her, but he didn't hold out much hope for a future that included her. It wasn't just the lying.

It was what his father might have done.

Chapter Seventeen

Danae poured coffee for a group of fishermen and tried to smile at their dated jokes. News of the murder hadn't gotten around just yet, and she was trying to appear normal. Most likely, one of the people she'd served coffee or pie had killed Jack. She couldn't help but think that if she observed everyone closely, maybe she'd be able to pick out the killer.

Sighing, she walked back behind the counter to start a new pot of coffee. Who was she kidding? If someone in Calais was a killer, that ability had been in them long before now, and she'd never noticed.

In the movies, it was always the person you least suspected, but in this case, she doubted that would apply. Amos wasn't capable of overpowering Jack even if his foot wasn't broken and even if Jack was passed out drunk. Carter, his mother and William were all on the list of least suspicious, but if it turned out to be one of them, she was packing her bags and moving to a remote cabin in Alaska where she never had to see people again. If her discernment was that poor, she needed to remain alone the rest of her life.

Johnny, the café owner, looked over at her as she refilled the coffeepot. His face was drawn and several shades lighter than normal. Carter had talked to him early that morning, so he was aware of the situation and didn't appear to be taking it very well.

"I still can't believe it," he said, his voice low. "It really happened, right?"

She nodded.

He blew out a breath. "Part of me keeps hoping Carter will come in here with that silly grin—you know the one—and tell me he was pulling my leg. But the other part of me knows Carter would never joke about something like this. It's just so hard to take in."

"I know. I'm having trouble processing it myself."

He looked across the half-empty café. "It's quiet now, but by lunchtime, it will get around. More people will show up, wanting the news. Heaven help me, I don't know that I can give it to them."

Danae placed her hand on Johnny's arm. "No one would fault you if you closed today, especially once they all find out what happened. Maybe you should do it before it gets busy."

"Thirty years I've owned this place and the only time I closed was for Hurricane Katrina," he mused. "Maybe you're right. I'll think on it while I scrub these pots. Got to keep moving so I can keep my mind off it."

He moved over to the double sink and started washing pots. Danae went back into the sitting area to clear dishes from the vacated tables. An elderly couple sat at a table near the door, and they were the only other occupants at the moment.

As she stacked the dishes in a plastic container, her mind raced. So many things had happened since last night, and she couldn't get them all sorted out. Her attacker, her night with Zach and Jack's murder all pushed and shoved, vying for her attention. If the murder didn't weigh so heavily on her, she might take time to marvel at the fact that her night with Zach didn't bother her like it would have a week ago.

That in itself should be enough to send her into a panic, but instead, the thought of the two of them, wrapped around each other on that lumpy bed, made her feel warm and safe. She'd never met someone who made her feel as if everything could be all right simply because they were there. Usually, her experience with people had been exactly the opposite, but with Zach, she'd gone places with her heart that she never expected to go.

As she was finishing up the second table, the bells on the front door jangled and Zach stepped inside. She smiled, already feeling better because he was there.

"Not busy, I see," he said.

"No. The breakfast rush happened early, and the news hasn't gotten around, yet. But it's only a matter of time. I'm trying to convince Johnny to close for the day. He's not taking Jack's death very well."

"That's probably not a bad idea." He pointed to a table in the corner. "Is it all right if I rent that booth for a while?"

"Make yourself comfortable. Do you want something to eat?"

"No, but a coffee would be great." He glanced around. "And if you can take a break, there's something I need to talk to you about."

"Okay." She headed back behind the counter and poured two coffees.

"I'm taking a break, Johnny."

He nodded. "Nothing going on anyway."

She carried the coffees over to the booth and slipped in across from him. "Are those the journals from Purcell's bedroom?" she asked, pointing to the notebooks he'd placed on the table.

"Yeah, I put the box in the backseat of your car and locked it. The back window on my truck's broken, and I didn't want to risk anyone stealing it."

"Good." If someone wanted the paperwork, then that meant they thought it contained something important. Maybe the answers they were looking for.

The bells over the café door jangled again and Danae looked up to see Carter enter. He didn't look happy. She jumped up from her seat.

"Is something wrong?" she asked.

"Yeah." He glanced at Zach then back at her.

She sat back down and Carter pulled a chair over to sit at the end of the booth.

"Yesterday," Carter began, "when I talked to that FBI agent who investigated Purcell-Lambert, we met at a coffee shop on Maxwell Street. A new bank building is going up across the street."

Carter's jaw flexed and he stared at Zach, whose eyes widened.

"You want to tell me," Carter said, "why you're here, posing as a handyman, when you own one of the biggest commercial construction companies in New Orleans?"

Danae sucked in a breath, feeling like a metal wrecking ball had just slammed into her chest. Surely Carter was mistaken.

But one look at the guilty expression Zach wore and she knew it was true.

"How could you?" she managed to ask, even more angry that her voice shook as she spoke.

Zach sighed. "I was about to tell you, I swear. That's what I wanted to talk to you about."

Danae glared at him, wondering why her instincts had let her down this way. She'd let him into her heart, and all this time, it had been a lie.

"You're going to tell me why you lied and pretended to care about me? This ought to be good."

"I do care about you. That's what made my lie even worse. I didn't want to hurt you, but I was afraid telling you the truth would hurt you even more."

"I don't see how."

"You owe her the truth," Carter said. "It's too late to worry about hurting her. That's already done. She deserves to know why."

Zach nodded. "My dad died a year ago. He was ill for a long time, and toward the end, he wasn't always lucid. But right before he passed, he awakened and told me he regretted something—told me like he was confessing before he died. The only thing I understood in his mumblings was your mother's name, Ophelia LeBeau."

"How did he know my mother?"

Zach shook his head. "I'd never heard the name before, but if you could have seen him— he was insane with worry. My father was a kind and gentle man. He raised me alone after my mom died. I've never even seen him raise his voice, but…"

"What did you father do for a living?"

"He was a funeral-home director."

"So maybe he handled Ophelia's funeral arrangements," Carter suggested.

"That's what I thought at first," Zach said, "but it bothered me so much, I did some digging. Around the time Ophelia passed, my dad made a large deposit into his personal checking account—twenty thousand dollars."

Danae gasped. "Just like the people paid to take us."

Zach nodded. "It gave me a start when you said there were four entries in that journal, but I looked at it this morning when you were in the shower and the dates for those payments are dated after the one my father deposited."

Zach opened one of the journals he'd brought into the café and pointed to a twenty-thousand-dollar entry. "That payment is dated five days before my father deposited the money. Look at the initials—D.S. My father's name was David."

"I still don't understand the problem," Danae said. "Purcell had to pay for the funeral."

Zach shook his head. "My father didn't own the funeral home. He was just the director. He would never deposit funeral money into his personal account, and if it was that aboveboard, it wouldn't have weighed so heavily on him at his death."

Carter's expression was grave. "I've wondered for a while if it's possible that Purcell killed Ophelia and made it look like an accident. But maybe that wasn't it at all. Maybe he killed her and simply paid off the people who would talk. Maybe that's why he was buying expensive art with estate money then turning around and selling it but with nothing to show for it personally."

"He was paying them to keep silent," Danae said, her stomach churning at Carter's suggestion that made so much sense.

She slid out of the booth. "I can't deal with this right now. You two can hash out the horrible details. I just need some time away from this—it's all too sordid."

She gave Zach a painful parting glance before crossing the café and entering the storeroom. Then the tears she'd been holding in burst through, and she sank down on the storeroom floor and cried so hard she thought she'd collapse from the effort.

All those years spent protecting herself,

and the one time she lowered her guard, it had brought her nothing but pain. She'd come to Calais looking for herself, but all she'd found were horrible actions and unbearable grief.

She pulled her legs up and circled her arms around them, wishing she'd never come home.

Zach watched as Danae walked away and he started to follow her, but Carter grabbed his arm and stopped him.

"Let her go," Carter said. "She's not ready to talk to you, or me, for that matter."

"I wasn't using her."

"I know," Carter said. "I could see it in your face. You care about her, but you hurt her. Probably more than anyone else except Purcell."

Zach stared at the table, feeling sick to his stomach. "Because she trusted me and that's something she never does." He looked up at Carter. "When my feelings for her started to change, I wanted to tell her, but then I was afraid she'd hate me—not for lying, but for what my father might have done. If he was involved…"

"I get it," Carter said. "That doesn't mean I condone the way you went about things, but I understand why you felt you had to."

"Do you think she'll ever forgive me?"

Carter shook his head. "It's hard to say as I don't really know her that well. If I had to guess, I'd say that eventually she will, but that doesn't mean she'll want to have anything to do with you."

Carter's words cut through Zach like a razor blade, but he knew the other man was only telling him the truth. And it wasn't anything Zach hadn't already thought, although he wasn't quite ready to face the potential finality.

"Sorry to interrupt." Johnny's voice sounded behind them. "Carter, I put together a container of soup and a casserole for your mom. I wanted to do something to help Cherise, but the only thing I'm good at is feeding people. I know your mother doesn't need any help cooking, but it's one less thing she'll have to see to—for a couple of meals, at least."

Zach looked up at the café owner and could tell the man wasn't taking Jack's murder well. He was pale and his voice and hands shook as he spoke.

"That's very considerate of you," Carter said, "and I'm sure my mom will appreciate it. Do you need me to deliver the stuff?"

"No, Danae's going to do it. I'm closing for the rest of the day, and she burned her arm getting the casserole out of the oven. Doc Broussard is at your mom's house right now, checking on Cherise, so Danae is going to deliver the food and have him take a look at the burn."

"Is it bad?" Zach asked, his stomach clutching at the thought of Danae in any more pain.

"No," Johnny assured him, "but I want Doc to take a look and give her something to put on it—injured on the job and all that." He tried to smile, but wasn't successful, then gave them a nod before shuffling back to the kitchen.

A shadow passed across the café's plate-glass window and Zach looked over in time to see Danae walk by on the sidewalk, carrying the food containers to her car. He clenched his hands, mentally forcing himself from jumping up from the table and running after her. She'd gone to the trouble of walking out the back door and around the building. Zach could only assume she'd done so to avoid looking at him.

He couldn't really blame her.

"Let's get out of here so Johnny can close," Carter said.

Zach rose from the booth and glanced around the café, just realizing it was completely empty aside from the two of them. He shook his head. He'd been so absorbed in the conversation and his own thoughts that he'd never even seen the older couple leave.

"I think we should talk to William," Carter said as they exited the café. "We can bring him up-to-date on your situation. He will know what arrangements were made for Ophelia's funeral and can probably gain access to Ophelia's autopsy reports."

Carter pulled out his cell phone and spoke briefly to the attorney.

"He's at his office," Carter said, "and can talk to us now."

"Great," Zach said, but he was already ashamed to tell the attorney how he'd lied. "Does he know about Jack?"

"Yeah. Given the circumstances, I thought it best that he be in the loop."

Zach nodded. "Do you think… Danae's all right going to your mother's house alone, right?"

"She'll be fine. Besides, Doc Broussard is there, too."

"Yeah, I guess so." But it didn't stop him from worrying, which was foolish. Three other adults were plenty of protection for Danae. More protection than him. The way things had turned out, he'd hurt her far more than the attacker.

Carter's cell phone rang and he pulled it from his pocket and answered it. The conversation was brief, but Zach could tell he was frustrated.

"That was the state police. They want me to meet them at the crime scene and answer some questions. I tried to keep them out of this, but with the potential connection to Alaina's attack, I couldn't. I've got to run but you go ahead and meet with William. Tell him everything."

"Good luck," Zach said.

Carter lifted one hand as he hurried away.

Zach watched him for a couple of seconds, delaying the inevitable. The last thing he wanted was to tell another person how he'd lied—tell another person that he suspected his father had been involved in something sordid. But it had to be done.

He'd opened Pandora's box by coming here. Now more people than just him were awaiting answers.

And if it was the last thing he did, he was going to see that they got them.

WILLAMINA TRAHAN LIVED at the end of a dead-end road, in a beautifully maintained farmhouse on five acres of cleared land, surrounded by the swamp. Her nearest neighbor was Carter, who lived a mile up the road from his mother. Danae drove slowly down the road to Willamina's house, trying to get a grip before she had to face the older woman. Willamina was one of the most observant and compassionate people Danae had ever met. One look at her right now, and Willamina would immediately know something was wrong. The last thing Danae wanted to do was dump her problems on Willamina when she already had her hands full caring for Cherise.

As she pulled into the driveway and parked next to Doc Broussard's car, she took a deep breath and practiced a smile. It looked more like a grimace, but maybe Willamina would be too distracted by everything else to notice. She gathered the food containers and made her way to the front door.

Not wanting to awaken Cherise if she was sleeping, she balanced the containers on her leg and rapped lightly with one hand. Footsteps sounded on the hardwood floors inside, and a couple of seconds later, Willamina opened the door and gave her a smile.

"Connie, come in." Willamina held the door open for her to enter.

"I'm sorry," Willamina said as she pointed to the kitchen. "I should be calling you Danae. With everything going on, it slipped my mind."

"That's all right," Danae said as she slid the containers onto the kitchen counter. "It will probably take everyone some time to get used to it all. How is Cherise?"

Willamina frowned. "Doc Broussard is in with her now. She seems physically okay, but I think she's in shock. Doc is going to try to talk to her. The state police are pushing for an interview. I know the sooner they get information, the more likely they are to catch whoever did this, but she's so fragile."

"I can't imagine finding Jack that way...."

"I can't, either. Would you like something to drink? I just brewed some sweet tea. I'm coffee'd out."

"That would be nice. Thank you."

Willamina prepared two glasses of sweet tea and pointed to the patio doors. "Let's take it outside. I could use some fresh air, and Doc Broussard may be in there awhile. Johnny said you burned yourself. How bad is it?"

Danae followed Willamina onto the patio and sank into one of the cushioned lawn chairs. "It's not bad at all. Johnny is just stressed over everything. He wants to do something, which is why he prepared the food, but I don't think he could face bringing it over himself."

"So he made an excuse to send you. Sounds like a typical male."

"I don't mind. I would have offered anyway. I talked Johnny into closing the café, and I don't really feel like sinking back into my own work at the moment."

Willamina handed her a glass of tea and sat in the chair next to her. "So are you going to tell me what's wrong or do I have to guess?"

Danae sighed. "I should have known I couldn't hide anything from you."

"I don't know why you tried. You know I'm

always here for anyone who needs to talk things out. Talking is my second-best skill."

"What's first?"

"Well, that depends on who you ask. I say listening is first, but Carter says it's giving unsolicited advice."

"Typical male." They both said it at the same time and Danae smiled.

"Carter's a good man," Danae said. "Whatever you did worked."

"A mother's work is never done, but at least I have Alaina to pull some of the weight. Now, why don't you tell me what man's got you riled?"

Danae shook her head, amazed again at Willamina's perception. "With everything going on in my life, how do you know it's man problems?"

Willamina patted her hand. "Oh, honey, I saw that look on your face when I opened the door. Only a man can cause that particular look of anger, frustration and heartbreak all at the same time."

"When you're right, you're right." She took a deep breath and started telling Willamina about Zach. It was easier than she'd thought it would be, and once she got started, she didn't stop until she'd laid the whole sordid mess at Willamina's feet.

Willamina listened intently the entire time,

never interrupting, but Danae could tell by her expression what she was thinking. When she finally ran out of words, Willamina leaned over and hugged her.

"The two of you are breaking my heart," she said.

"The two of us?"

Willamina released her and nodded. "Here you are with a stolen childhood and that wall of steel you put up around yourself, then the one man who managed to scale it is at the precipice of having everything he thought he knew about his childhood destroyed."

Danae frowned. She hadn't really thought about Zach that way, but what Willamina said made sense. He must be horribly worried that the father he loved and thought he knew wasn't the man Zach thought he was.

"I'm struggling to find my identity," Danae said, "and he's struggling not to lose his."

Willamina looked pleased. "That's it exactly. Now, you and I both know that even if Zach's father was involved in something nefarious all those years ago, that's no reflection on the man Zach is today. Nor is it, in my opinion, a reflection on what kind of father he was to Zach, but he's not likely to see it that way. Not yet."

"He's just thinking it's all a lie."

"Yes, but it's more than that."

"What do you mean?"

"Now he's also afraid that his father was involved in the worst thing that ever happened to the woman he loves."

Danae stared at Willamina. "Loves? No, he doesn't... He can't... I barely know him."

"I knew an hour after I met Carter's father that he was the one."

Her mind raced, trying to process Willamina's words. "Even if that's true and his father did something wrong, that doesn't have anything to do with Zach. I would never hold that against him."

Willamina gave her a sad smile. "I know that, dear, but he doesn't. So he got scared and made a foolish mistake—he hid the truth from you. I don't agree with his method, but I do understand the thought process behind it."

Danae reached over to squeeze Willamina's hand, as the older woman had done to her earlier. "How did you get so smart?"

"My mama was a pistol. I got it all from her. She would have loved you."

Tears welled up in Danae's eyes, and before she could get control of them, they spilled over onto her face.

Willamina rose from her chair and leaned over to kiss the top of Danae's head. "You sit here for a while with your thoughts. I've got to run into Calais real quick and drop off the church keys to Celia. Someone else is going to have to run the bake sale this afternoon. I'm needed here."

Danae sniffed and wiped the tears from her face with her hand. "Thank you. For everything."

"I'll tell Doc Broussard you need to see him before he leaves. I'll be back in fifteen minutes or so." She gave Danae's shoulder a squeeze before walking away.

Willamina's car started up a minute later, and Danae heard it pull away. She stared into the swamp, wondering how her previously simple life had gotten so complicated. A minute later, she rose and strolled across the backyard, taking in the layers of texture and color that Willamina had worked into her landscape. The woman had a real gift for design.

As she neared the side of the house, she heard a tinkling sound from the front yard, like the sound of glass breaking. Without thinking, she rushed around the side of the house and almost collided with the man standing next to her car and holding a crowbar.

Chapter Eighteen

William must have been watching for him, because he opened the front door of the law office as Zach approached.

"Carter had to go meet the state police," Zach explained, "but I'm supposed to bring you up to speed."

"Of course, come in." William waved a hand toward his office. "I'm going to lock this so that no one interrupts us. I'm not really open on Saturdays, but it doesn't stop people from dropping by if they think I'm here."

"No, I guess it wouldn't." The attorney was one of those likable father-figure types. Zach could imagine that most of Calais's residents had probably stopped in at some time or another for advice.

Zach slid into a chair in front of William's antique desk as the attorney took a seat behind it. Deciding it was best to simply lay everything out on the table, Zach told William everything—

his father's deathbed confession and Zach's real reason for coming to Calais. Then he showed the attorney Purcell's journals and explained the entry matching the time line and amount of the deposit his father made.

"I can't think of any legitimate reason," Zach said, "that my father would have been paid by Purcell."

The grave look on the attorney's face let Zach know the older man thought the situation looked as dire as Zach did.

"Yes, well," William said, "I can see why you'd find that troubling. You said your father was a funeral director. Did he deal with the preparation of the bodies?"

"No, but he knew a lot about it. I guess you pick up things after so many years."

William nodded. "Quite so, I'm sure, but would it be enough for him to notice if something weren't appropriate?"

"You mean something the embalmer didn't notice?"

"Not necessarily. We've already found evidence of Purcell paying different people for less-than-desirable services. It could be that he paid off the embalmer as well as your father."

"That hadn't occurred to me," Zach said, the one sliver of hope that his father hadn't involved himself in something horrible completely slipping away.

"The only thing," Zach continued, "worth paying an embalmer and funeral director to lie about is murder. You, me, Carter…we've all danced around the word, but we're all thinking it."

The sympathy on the attorney's face was clear. "Yes, I'm afraid you're right."

"Carter wanted you to get a copy of the autopsy. I guess he's hoping we could find something the medical examiner missed."

"An autopsy wasn't performed."

Zach stared. "What? Why not?"

"There was no suspicion of foul play. Ophelia had been to see a doctor in New Orleans just two days before, complaining of chest pains and being short of breath. The doctor did a cursory exam and concluded she had pneumonia and requested she come back for further testing after the pneumonia had run its course."

"So everyone assumed she died from the pneumonia."

"That or she had an underlying heart condition that was exacerbated by the pneumonia."

Zach shook his head, something about it all still not adding up. "But Ophelia was a young woman. I still can't imagine a coroner making such a leap."

"It wasn't the coroner who made it," William said. "The only coroner back then was in New Orleans."

"Then who would have called the death?"

"The local doctor."

A wave of panic ran through Zach. "Doc Broussard?"

William's eyes widened and he nodded. "He's been the only doctor here for a good forty years. Oh, my…I never thought…"

Zach jumped up from his chair. "Call Carter and tell him to get to his mother's house. Danae is there…with Doc Broussard."

William's face paled as he reached for the phone. Zach tore out of the office and jumped into his truck, cursing himself for putting the box of papers in Danae's car. Killing Jack had already given away his level of desperation. He wouldn't stop at killing again to keep his secret hidden.

GLASS FROM THE broken car window glinted in the gravel driveway, leaving her no doubt as to what had happened, but she was floored by the man himself, former sheriff Roger Martin.

"You?" She took a step back from him, but he grabbed her arm, preventing her from escaping. "But why?"

"You meddling little bitch." He pulled a pistol from his waistband and opened the car door. "Give me the keys and get in."

Danae scrambled to come up with an alternative escape. If she cried out, Doc Broussard might hear her, but Martin had a clear shot at him when he came out of the house. Her cell phone was sitting on the back patio, of no use to her, and her pistol was in her purse, sitting on Willamina's kitchen counter.

A glance around the lawn didn't reveal Martin's car, but the bayou ran behind Willamina's house, just past the cleared land. He could have easily taken his boat here in order to gain entry to the property unobserved.

"I don't have the keys," she lied, trying to stall. "They're inside."

"I see them in your pocket. Give them to me, or I shoot you here."

One look at the pure hatred and rage in his expression, and Danae knew he wasn't joking. If she fought back, Doc Broussard and Cherise might hear, or Willamina might return. The only way she could ensure their safety was to leave with the man she was certain had killed Jack.

She pulled the keys from her pocket and handed them to him before sliding into the car, her tennis shoes crunching on the broken glass on the floorboard. Martin hurried around the front of the car, keeping his pistol trained on her, and climbed into the driver's side. As he backed up, Willamina's front door opened and Doc Broussard looked out.

"Get down!" Martin yelled before Danae could signal for help.

He grabbed her hair and yanked her down in the seat. At the same time, he punched the accelerator, and the car launched forward, the spray of gravel pinging against the car's under-carriage and sides.

Danae crouched on the floorboard, her head pounding where Martin had yanked her hair. "Where are you taking me?"

"Home to the LeBeau estate. Where it all began and where it's all going to end."

"What are you going to do?"

"Something I should have done as soon as Purcell died. Burn it to the ground."

"What you're looking for is in that box in the backseat."

He looked down at her and sneered. "That's not all I was looking for, and I'm not about to risk that you found everything implicating me. Purcell was crazy. Who knows what kind of scribbled ramblings he has shoved into that mountain of crap in that house."

"You're not going to get away with this."

He laughed. "Of course I am. I've gotten

away with it all this time. If that idiot Jack had done his job properly, you wouldn't be in this position. Blame him for your early demise. But when everyone hears the sad and damaged heiress burned herself down in the house, they're not going to blink."

Danae's stomach turned. Martin wasn't even on the list of their suspects. No one would have any reason to connect him with the fire. Except for the remote chance that Doc Broussard got a glimpse of him as he drove away, Martin was right—he was going to get away with everything.

"Purcell killed my mother, didn't he? And you covered it up. You and the coroner and the funeral director and God only knows who else."

"You'll never know, and neither will anyone else when I'm done. I should have known better than to trust Purcell. He's managed to screw us all from the grave."

The car dropped down into a rut and her head slammed into the center console, blurring her vision. She closed her eyes, hoping the blurring cleared before they got to the house. The last thing she intended to do was go quietly inside to be lit on fire.

If she was going down, she was going down with a fight.

Sitting on the patio with Willamina, Danae

had felt cheated by life once more, sad and angry over what she'd viewed as betrayal by Zach. But Willamina had put things in perspective…reminded her that most people tried to hide the parts of their past they weren't proud of.

Despite all his suspicions, Zach had helped her continue her search of the records. He'd put himself at risk to protect her, knowing all the while that what she was doing might lead to the worst possible information about his own father. Last night had been real. Someone who'd been faking her entire life recognized the difference. It was thrilling and frightening, but more than anything, she didn't want it to be over.

At any other time, the drive from Calais to the estate would have seemed to take forever, but this time, it felt like only a few minutes. When the car screeched to a halt, Danae started to rise, but Martin pointed the gun back at her.

"Not so quick, sweetheart." He reached into his pocket with his free hand and tossed a set of handcuffs onto the floorboard. "Put those on."

Her heart sank as she clicked the metal around her wrists, eliminating any possibility of gaining the upper hand in a fight. Even her ability to run was seriously compromised. There was nothing left to do but go along with him for the time being and watch closely for an opportunity to escape.

And pray.

ZACH'S TRUCK SLID to a stop in front of Willamina's house and he jumped out, his pistol clenched in his right hand. Before he reached the front door, Doc Broussard opened it and hurried outside.

"Hold it right there," Zach said and pointed his gun at the doctor.

Doc Broussard's face paled and his eyes widened, as he froze in place. "What in the world is wrong with you?"

"What did you do with Danae?"

"I didn't do anything with her. I was with Cherise when I heard a commotion outside. When I looked out, Danae's car was racing away."

"She figured out it was you, didn't she?"

"What was me? You're beginning to worry me."

"You knew Purcell murdered Ophelia. You called her death natural causes so that there wouldn't be an autopsy."

Doc Broussard's jaw dropped and he stared at Zach for several seconds. "Murdered?"

Zach studied the other man closely, but if he was acting, he was really good at it. "Yes, murdered. Purcell's been paying for the cover-up for years, including your part."

Doc Broussard shook his head, the disbelief clear in his expression. "But I didn't pronounce Ophelia. I'd broken my leg hunting—"

"Damn!" Suddenly, everything snapped together and the picture was clear.

"Was she alone in the car?"

"I... It looked like two people, but I couldn't be sure."

"Call Carter," he yelled at the stunned doctor. "Tell him everything."

"Wait! Where are you going?"

"I've got to find Danae before Roger Martin kills her."

Chapter Nineteen

Zach slammed his truck in Reverse, then floored it down the gravel road, his mind processing all the pieces that had just fallen neatly into place. Doc Broussard had told them the story about breaking his leg hunting, and how he knew something hit him, but no tracks or weapon had been found. It was the sheriff who'd searched the woods.

Sheriff Roger Martin.

He'd claimed he found nothing, but Zach would bet anything it was because Martin was the one who'd clocked Doc Broussard. With the doctor out of the way, the sheriff would have called Ophelia's death.

All those years ago, those men had staged the perfect crime. If Trenton Purcell hadn't insisted on keeping records, Roger Martin might have gone to the grave without anyone the wiser.

Like his dad.

Zach clenched his jaw, pushing that thought

to the back of his mind. It was something he'd have to find a way to deal with, but that could wait. First, he had to save Danae.

If Doc Broussard saw two people in her car, he had no doubt the other was Martin, but where would he take her? In fact, the documents Martin wanted were in the backseat of Danae's car, so why take her at all? The only thing Zach could figure was that she caught him trying to take the documents.

So if he had the documents, where was he taking her now?

The house!

The answer came to him in a flash and he cursed himself for being so stupid. There could be other documents in the house that implicated Martin. He would have to return to the house and make sure those documents were never found.

He punched the accelerator down and gripped the steering wheel with both hands, struggling to keep the car from jolting off the cavity-filled road. Never had the drive to the house seemed longer or the road in worse shape than right now, and he prayed he wasn't too late.

Martin had no idea anyone was onto him. He wouldn't hesitate to eliminate Danae if he thought she was his only living threat. Zach would bet money that was exactly what happened to Jack.

He stopped just short of the house, figuring if Martin didn't know he was there, he would have the advantage. Hoping like hell the window he'd released was still unlocked, he ran through the patch of swamp between the road and the house. He approached from the side, praying they were in Purcell's office, where no windows existed.

Danae's car was parked in the center of the drive in front of the main entry. Shards from the broken window glinted in the sunlight, giving Zach a good idea of what Danae had walked up on.

He didn't even hesitate before running across the small open area to the side of the house. Gripping the window with both hands, he eased it up, trying not to make any noise. The window stuck a couple of times, but he pushed a bit harder and managed to get it up enough to crawl inside.

He raced to the doorway and stopped to listen. Faint scuffling sounded on the second floor, but not directly above him. His instincts had been right. They were in Purcell's office. He slipped out of the bedroom and flattened himself against the wall, careful to stay well below the second-floor balcony. He paused directly below Purcell's office only long enough to ascertain that Martin was up there, then continued along the wall until he reached the hallway to the laundry room.

He couldn't approach the office from the balcony without being seen, but if he took the servants' stairs into Purcell's bedroom, he might be able to get the jump on Martin. He had no doubt the other man had a gun—otherwise Danae would have fought him at Willamina's—so he had to be careful. The last thing he wanted was for Danae to be injured in the cross fire.

The door to the servants' stairs opened without a sound, further convincing Zach that Martin or Jack had been in residence when he and Danae were in the house. The hinges were well-oiled, and none of the wooden steps were loose—a far cry from the condition of the rest of the house.

He stopped at the top of the stairs and put his ear to the door, trying to determine whether anyone was in the bedroom. The noises he heard didn't sound as if they were right on the other side of the door, but with the high ceilings and impossible drafts, it was hard to be certain.

Taking a deep breath, he cracked open the door and peered out into the dim bedroom. What he could see of the room was empty, so he widened the crack enough to see the entry to the office. The light from the balcony streamed into the office, giving it more illumination than the dank bedroom. It was just enough light to create shadows.

Zach waited until the shadows moved, then eased the door open wide enough to slip into the bedroom. He crept across the bedroom floor to the office entry and listened, trying to gauge Martin's position in the room.

"Where is the money?" Martin asked. "I know Purcell hid the cash somewhere in here."

"I didn't find any cash," Danae said.

"Lying whore. I know what you are, with your thrift-shop clothes and your cheap haircut. You hid the money for yourself. Now tell me where it is!"

"Even if I had it, why would I tell you? You're going to kill me anyway. Just get on with it. Set the place on fire and burn me down with your blood money."

Zach's stomach clenched and he gripped his pistol tighter. Martin's plan was perfect, but he'd been mistaken on one key element—that Danae had people who loved her and were hot on his trail.

He couldn't tell by the voices where either Martin or Danae were positioned in the office, but he couldn't wait any longer. It was a risk he'd have to take. Clutching his pistol in the ready position, he sprang around the corner and came face-to-face with the worst possible scenario.

Martin stood in the doorway between the office and the balcony, his gun pointed directly at Danae, who stood handcuffed in the middle of the office, facing Zach. He didn't have a clear shot at Martin, and Martin could shoot a lot quicker than Danae could duck.

"Well, what do we have here?" Martin said. "Looks like the heiress has a rescuer. What a shame that he's not better suited for the job. Now, I want you to put your pistol on the desk and step back or your girlfriend takes one to the head. You don't want to see that, do you?"

The blood rushed from Danae's face and Zach's trigger finger twitched, aching for the clear shot that simply wasn't going to come. He didn't doubt for a moment that Martin would do exactly what he threatened, but even if Zach complied, he had no doubt the end result would be the same.

If he dived and attempted a shot, at least he had a chance. If he put his pistol on the desk, it was all over.

He looked at Danae, hoping she understood what he was about to do and why. Hoping she had some idea of what she meant to him. A single tear ran down her cheek and she gave him an almost imperceptible nod. He clenched the pistol and prepared to dive.

But before he could act, a shimmering light appeared above them, bright as a spotlight and growing in size.

"What the hell?" Martin shouted. "What kind of trick is this? Do what I say now or I kill you both right here."

A crackle of electricity broke through the room, flashing so bright it was as if lightning had struck right there inside the office. Zach put his free hand up to shield himself from the brightness and saw hands reach out from the light and shove Danae to the ground.

He couldn't see through the light at all, but instantly, Zach fired at the doorway. Martin yelled and Zach fired again and again, praying that he'd at least managed to disarm him.

He heard the crack of wood, like a branch splintering, a scream and then a loud thud. The crackle of electricity vanished as quickly as it came, and the light began to fade. Zach rushed out of the office to the broken railing and looked over. A growing pool of blood seeped from under Martin's head, matching the three holes in his chest.

Zach ran back into the office and sank down onto the floor to gather Danae in his arms.

"Look," she whispered and pointed to the fading light.

Zach looked over and gasped. Inside the light was the figure of a woman. She wore a long white gown and smiled at Danae before fading completely away.

"It was my mother," Danae said. "The two of you saved me."

"I was so afraid I'd lost you."

"I was afraid, too, but somewhere deep down, I knew you'd come for me. I've never felt that with someone before. I was scared of the feelings."

"You don't have to explain."

"No, but I have to say this—I don't blame you for hiding the truth when you came to Calais. I wanted to be upset, but the reality is, I did the same thing. I understand your reasons, and I want you to know that I don't hold you responsible for anything your father might have done. His choices were his own."

The great weight on Zach's shoulders disappeared in an instant. The past troubled him, and probably always would, but it didn't compare to the worry he'd had that the only person who mattered to his future might not be able to reconcile the past with the future.

"I tried to avoid my feelings, too," Zach said, "but somewhere along the line, I fell in love with you. When I saw you standing there, with that gun pointed at you, it was as if my entire life were over. I don't want to be without you, Danae."

"I don't want to be without you, either."

He cupped his hands around her face and leaned over to gently kiss her.

So much work remained—working for the estate, uncovering the past—but with Danae in his arms and his heart, Zach knew it would be okay.

Epilogue

One month later

Danae clutched Zach's hand as they waited outside of William Duhon's law office for Alaina and Carter, who were crossing the street. Alaina lifted her hand to wave at them and Danae smiled and waved back with her free hand, marveling at how much her life had changed in thirty days.

Carter, along with the state police, investigated everything and found the weapon used to murder Jack in Roger Martin's boat. He'd tried to clean it off, but his fingerprints were right there, along with microscopic traces of Jack's blood. Based on the way things turned out and Danae's account of Martin saying Jack paid for his incompetence, the state police were happy to mark the file solved and get back to New Orleans.

Danae finished out her two weeks in her cabin

with Zach at her side and in her bed. Alaina returned days after Zach killed Roger Martin, and the two sisters had spent long hours talking about their past, present and future. Danae was amazed at how quickly her attachment to Alaina had formed and now couldn't imagine a life without her sister. Both of them prayed daily that William would locate Joelle soon, as she was the missing piece that would make everything whole.

If anyone had told Danae when she came to Calais that she'd acquire a family and a fortune, she would have laughed. Of the two, she was happiest with the family.

She'd talked at length with Zach and Alaina about what happened that day in the office— about what she and Zach saw in the light. Danae was certain it was her mother and could still feel her mother's hands on her, pushing her out of harm's way. Alaina, normally focused only on facts and proof, didn't hesitate to believe everything they said. They'd spent many hours in the house since then, hoping that their mother would appear to them again, but it seemed as if she'd vanished as quickly as she'd appeared.

She continued her work for William but so far hadn't found anything that shed more light on her mother's death or how Zach's father was involved. But she'd already promised she wouldn't stop looking until she'd reviewed every last sheet of paper in the house.

Beginning next week, that review would take place in Zach's flat in New Orleans so that Zach could return to his real-life responsibilities of managing huge construction projects. They'd spend weekends in Calais, working on the house, continuing the inventory work and spending time with Alaina and Carter.

Then next spring, Danae would start culinary school, fulfilling a lifelong dream.

Despite what they were about to do, Danae couldn't keep herself from grinning as Alaina stepped onto the sidewalk and gave Danae and Zach a hug. Carter shook Zach's hand and kissed Danae's cheek. All of them looked a little nervous.

"Are you sure you want to do this?" Carter asked.

Alaina slipped her hand into Danae's and squeezed as she studied her sister's face and nodded.

"We're sure," Danae said.

Carter opened the door to the law office so they could enter. "Then let's go make it happen."

The secretary was expecting them and directed them straight to William's office. The attorney jumped up from his chair and hurried over to greet them, a big smile on his face.

"It's so good to see all of you…and especially together," William said. "Ophelia would have been pleased with her daughters' choices in men." He sniffed and took his seat, waving at them to sit in the chairs in front of the desk.

"When I heard you all wanted to speak to me," William said after they were seated, "I couldn't imagine what it was about. Something good, I hope? Marriage-license information? Joint retirement accounts?"

Zach and Carter glanced at each other, looking a bit uncomfortable, and Alaina laughed. "You're going to scare them out of here, William. Besides, Willamina has already claimed control of all till-death-do-us-part stuff."

William smiled. "Then I'll leave her to it. I learned a long time ago not to step into women's territory, especially Willamina's. So if it's not couples' business, what can I help you with?"

Danae looked over at Alaina. "Go ahead," she said. This was legal business, and she wanted her sister the attorney to take the lead.

"It depends on your definition of *good,*" Alaina said, "but we do think it's necessary."

William nodded. "I'll do my best to provide anything you need."

Alaina reached over for Danae's hand once

more, and Danae could feel her sister's hand trembling as she clutched her own.

"We want to exhume our mother."

* * * * *

Look for the heart-stopping conclusion of Jana DeLeon's miniseries
MYSTERE PARISH:
FAMILY INHERITANCE *when*
THE REUNION *goes on sale next month.*
You can find it wherever
Harlequin Intrigue books are sold!

LARGER-PRINT BOOKS!
GET 2 FREE LARGER-PRINT NOVELS PLUS 2 FREE GIFTS!

♦ HARLEQUIN®

INTRIGUE®

BREATHTAKING ROMANTIC SUSPENSE

YES! Please send me 2 FREE LARGER-PRINT Harlequin Intrigue® novels and my 2 FREE gifts (gifts are worth about $10). After receiving them, if I don't wish to receive any more books, I can return the shipping statement marked "cancel." If I don't cancel, I will receive 6 brand-new novels every month and be billed just $5.49 per book in the U.S. or $5.99 per book in Canada. That's a saving of at least 13% off the cover price! It's quite a bargain! Shipping and handling is just 50¢ per book in the U.S. and 75¢ per book in Canada.* I understand that accepting the 2 free books and gifts places me under no obligation to buy anything. I can always return a shipment and cancel at any time. Even if I never buy another book, the two free books and gifts are mine to keep forever.

199/399 HDN F42Y

Name _____
(PLEASE PRINT)

Address _____ Apt. # _____

City _____ State/Prov. _____ Zip/Postal Code _____

Signature (if under 18, a parent or guardian must sign) _____

Mail to the **Harlequin® Reader Service:**
IN U.S.A.: P.O. Box 1867, Buffalo, NY 14240-1867
IN CANADA: P.O. Box 609, Fort Erie, Ontario L2A 5X3

Are you a subscriber to Harlequin Intrigue books and want to receive the larger-print edition?
Call 1-800-873-8635 today or visit www.ReaderService.com.

* Terms and prices subject to change without notice. Prices do not include applicable taxes. Sales tax applicable in N.Y. Canadian residents will be charged applicable taxes. Offer not valid in Quebec. This offer is limited to one order per household. Not valid for current subscribers to Harlequin Intrigue Larger-Print books. All orders subject to credit approval. Credit or debit balances in a customer's account(s) may be offset by any other outstanding balance owed by or to the customer. Please allow 4 to 6 weeks for delivery. Offer available while quantities last.

Your Privacy—The Harlequin® Reader Service is committed to protecting your privacy. Our Privacy Policy is available online at www.ReaderService.com or upon request from the Harlequin Reader Service.

We make a portion of our mailing list available to reputable third parties that offer products we believe may interest you. If you prefer that we not exchange your name with third parties, or if you wish to clarify or modify your communication preferences, please visit us at www.ReaderService.com/consumerchoice or write to us at Harlequin Reader Service Preference Service, P.O. Box 9062, Buffalo, NY 14269. Include your complete name and address.

HILP13R

Reader Service.com

Manage your account online!

- Review your order history
- Manage your payments
- Update your address

---

*We've designed
the Harlequin® Reader Service
website just for you.*

Enjoy all the features!

- Reader excerpts from any series
- Respond to mailings and
  special monthly offers
- Discover new series available to you
- Browse the Bonus Bucks catalog
- Share your feedback

Visit us at:

ReaderService.com

RS13